Sharon's Shorts

A Multi-Genre Collection of Short Stories

Cover designed by Sharon K Connell
Images courtesy of Pixaby
Editing Services provided by Above the Pages

All Scripture is from the King James Authorized Version 1611

Sharon K Connell
Visit my website at www.authorsharonkconnell.com

Printed in the United States of America

First Printing: November 2020

ISBN-13 978-1-7329237-4-4

This book is dedicated to my Lord Jesus Christ who has enabled me to come up with the stories, led me to those who have assisted me through the creation and polishing of these tales, given me the ability to write, and guided me through the process.

Acknowledgements

My Thanks to all listed on this page for their contributions to the details of each story with professional information, critiques, support, and so much more. I am ever so grateful.

ACFW Scribes Critique Group

Arnold C. Hauswald, U.S. Army (Ret.)

Faye Hamilton, RN, over 30 years as an ER Trauma Nurse

Pam Lagomarsino of Above the Pages Editing Services

The International Writing Program from the University of Iowa and all the teachers and instructors who challenged me to create a number of these stories.

And whatsoever ye do in word or deed, do all in the name of the Lord Jesus, giving thanks to God and the Father by him. COLOSSIANS 3:17

Sharon's Shorts

A Multi-Genre Collection of Short Stories

Sharon K Connell

To Jeff.
Hope these stories lift your spirit.
Your friend
[illegible]

Ring-A-Ling
Holiday Blues

Ring-A-Ling Holiday Blues

First published in *Tales of Texas, Short Stories, Vol. 2, An Anthology of Texas Fiction,* Copyright © 2018, Publisher : Houston Writers House; 1st Edition (December 10, 2018)

Genre: Romance

Traci has volunteered to work at the jewelry store on Black Friday since she won't get to see her friend David who's moving from Houston to New York for a better job. Her heart is broken. He's not given her any sign of interest other than as a friend. Will she ever see him again? One situation after another adds further sorrow to her holiday. If only the wooden snowman outside her window were the real Frosty, and he was able to grant wishes.

Ring-A-Ling Holiday Blues

Houston, Texas

What? Ohhh...the alarm. Already? "Nooo, not already." Traci Winterhaven slapped at the clock on the nightstand until she struck the button. Ah, silence.

What had she been thinking? Busiest shopping day of the year and she had volunteered to work. Crazy people darting here and there. Tempers flaring for no good reason. At least she worked in a jewelry store in an exclusive downtown Houston mall, and not Wal-Mart with its herd of shoppers on Black Friday. That frenzy would be a nightmare.

She winced. Her dream last night was gut-wrenching enough when David said they wouldn't meet again. And then, *poof*—he vanished. Same thing she had dreamed every night since he told her about his job offer in New York—and that he'd accepted. *I hate soggy pillows.*

Traci rolled over. Her reaction might be understandable if they were engaged, but he'd never even mentioned marriage. Never kissed her either. Not that way, anyway. They were just friends...wonderful friends. Friends who never dated anyone else.

"Who are you kidding?" She loved that tall Texan. Had for some time now. But he was too busy with his career to develop any relationship. This year, she wouldn't get to spend even part of Christmas with him, thanks to his schedule.

Would David have time to keep in touch with her when he moved to New York and started his new life? How could she say goodbye?

With a moan, she slid her reluctant legs over the edge of the bed and tucked her feet into fuzzy black slippers. She grasped her plush purple bathrobe from the cedar chest at the foot of her bed and flipped it onto her shoulders. "Move, feet!"

Her body demanded she return to the nice warm bed and comforter.

"Come on. Move!" She shuffled to the window and tugged open the drapes. Even they seemed unwilling to cooperate on this frigid morning. When they did, her hand snapped up to shield her eyes from the sun's glare on fresh-fallen snow. "Wow! That bright light could blind a person."

The local weatherman had been right. Last night's temperature had fallen to freezing as predicted, but he hadn't mentioned an overnight snowfall.

Lots of caffeine. That was what she needed.

Traci shaded her eyes as her sight traveled to the neighbor's yard and the wooden snowman they'd set up next to the driveway. She chuckled. Still there, stovepipe hat and all.

Every year, Gramps had worn that tall black hat when he'd drive from his farm to her parents' home in Chicago after the first snow. Then he'd help her build the first snowman of the season. Her face contorted. When Gramps died from a heart attack, she was only twelve. How she missed him.

She took in a sharp breath. Now Grandma, Mom, and Dad were gone. They'd all passed on within a couple years of each other. Right before Christmas. Not a good time of the year for her. It didn't seem as if it would ever feel like Christmas again.

But thanks to her friend, Cynthia, David Lovejoy had come into her life. A smile came to Traci's lips. What a difference he'd made in only a year. Gramps would've loved him.

She winked at the snowman. Good thing she'd spotted that topper while she helped Grandma set aside clothes for the Salvation Army last year. "Right, Frosty?"

Was he smiling back? Wait, he had faced the street yesterday. The kids must have turned him.

Her gaze remained on Frosty as she mused. She'd also salvaged Gramps' silvery-blue winter scarf and that crazy, curved, black plastic pipe he'd always pretended to smoke while he read in his recliner. A sigh escaped. If he'd actually smoked a pipe in the house, Grandma would've had a hissy-fit. Traci grinned.

Yesterday had been an enjoyable day though. It was fun helping the three neighbor kids decorate the snowman with her grandfather's things. She leaned against the window frame.

As she pulled her robe tighter, the preteen triplets came bounding out of their house next door and scooped snow together with their hands. What were they doing...building a sandcastle from snow? A snowman...possibly? They hadn't a clue how to form a snowball, much less a whole man.

Their dad emerged from the side door of the home, feet slipping from one edge to the other as he made his way down the porch steps.

At the bottom, he landed on his derriere. He clutched the rail, stood, and brushed the snow from his backside. Traci laughed.

Mr. Richards continued on to his kids. He rolled a ball of snow on the ground, making it larger with each pass of the house, and gathering dead leaves in the process. *Clearly, he* wasn't born in the south and knew what he was doing. But there wouldn't be enough snow in the entire neighborhood to create a snowman as tall as their wooden Frosty. Perhaps a little brother instead.

Frosty stared at her with lifeless, black eyes.

How did that song go about Frosty the Snowman? "Fro-o-os-ty...the Snowman...was a—" Was he able to grant wishes? If so, she'd wish that David would ask her to marry him so she could join him in New York.

She pushed herself off the window frame with her shoulder. *Dream on.* If she were a stunning redhead like Cynthia, he'd ask in a heartbeat.

Did that snowman wink at me? Lack of sleep did the weirdest things.

Traci backed away from the window, leaving Frosty to supervise the kids and their dad in making him a brother. She crossed the plush carpet into the bathroom. "You need a shower."

One hour and five cups of coffee later, Traci stood behind a low glass counter with her patented jewelry-store-clerk smile in place, ready for the onslaught of Black Friday shoppers. *So, it begins.* She bent over the counter and looked between the ring cases into the mirrored shelf to make a quick check of her makeup. Tired blue eyes blinked at her. As she straightened, a long blonde lock of wavy hair fell to her right cheek. Annoying, persistent curl. She tucked it behind her ear.

Her boss opened the doors to a group of excited bargain-hunters who had huddled outside in the mall. Those limited-quantity advertised specials would go fast.

The first customer approached. Too young to want an engagement ring, she hoped.

A grin spread across the young man's face. "Hi. I'm looking for an engagement ring."

Her heart squeezed. Wonderful! Just wonderful. Would she ever wear one? Now that David was leaving, would she even want to marry anyone else?

The young man directed his attention to the jewels in the case. "It has to be the most beautiful ring ever. She's the most perfect girl in the world."

"Of course she is." Boy, he had it bad. "Not to worry. We have a large collection of exquisite rings from which you can choose. Yellow or white gold?"

With her best smile plastered on, she unlocked the display case and pulled out a tray of sparkling diamond rings from a lower shelf. When she lifted it to the counter, an empty space caught her eye. Someone must have bought the marquise engagement ring she'd admired from her first day in the shop—the most gorgeous ring in the store with its side stones and Celtic knot band. She'd never see it again—yet another Christmastime disappointment.

Throughout the morning, customers flowed in and out. Finally, she'd get a break. Traci sat on a high stool behind the display, slipped off her heels one at a time, and rubbed each foot against the calf of her leg. She wasn't sure she could deal with another customer looking for that special ring. Or another couple lost in their own world of romantic bliss.

Her cheeks ached from the pasted-on smile. *There should be a law against Black Friday Christmas shopping.*

She glanced at her watch. Lunchtime. Traci grabbed her purse from the bottom of the showcase and strolled into the mall. As she dodged shoppers, the phone conversation she had with David two days ago came to mind. She hadn't seen him for close to a week when he called while on break at the hospital. As soon as he spoke, she sensed something was wrong.

"I have to leave for New York this coming Monday, Traci. Before I start my new job, I have to find an apartment and settle in."

Her eyes burned as she entered McConnor's Grill in the next wing of the mall. She blinked tears away and seated herself next to the window that looked out toward people who hurried past like fish in an aquarium.

Would he come back to Texas? If he found a place to live, he might just send for his things. Was that why he'd made no Christmas plans? Nothing to keep him here since he had no family left in Houston.

She'd have to pick up a farewell gift after work while she did her Christmas shopping. What should she give him to show how much he meant to her? She stared out the window of the restaurant, her mind blank.

A waitress stepped to her side. "Have you decided what you want?"

"Yes, I'll have the chicken salad sandwich with fries and a glass of water. Thank you."

Traci's gaze returned to the mall shoppers as the server left with her order. Why hadn't David become more serious? What was wrong with her? Her dim reflection in the glass peered back. Wasn't she pretty enough? He'd often complimented her, how he loved the way she wore her hair clipped behind her ears and how it fell across her shoulders. He had even told her he'd never seen crystal blue eyes like hers. They'd gotten along great, had interesting conversations, and laughed. What was it then?

The waitress set the plate of food in front of her. Traci jerked. How long had she been daydreaming?

As she lifted a French fry to her mouth, movement in front of a store opposite the restaurant caught her eye. David? *With Cynthia?* They stopped, faced each other, and smiled. David gave her a tight hug. Then they left, laughing.

Tears flooded Traci's eyes. "So, that's it," she whispered. Why hadn't they told her about their relationship? Shapely, gorgeous, auburn-haired Cynthia had been the best friend she'd ever had since moving to Texas.

Traci pulled a tissue from her purse and dabbed at the tears. She picked up the sandwich. Her stomach lurched at the scent of chicken and mayonnaise as it neared her mouth. She dropped the food to the plate and pushed it away. *Would Cynthia go to New York with him?*

With a forced smile on her lips, Traci returned to the jewelry store.

A few minutes later, Cynthia breezed through the front door with a glow on her face. Traci's heart slid to her empty stomach. What was she doing here? She was supposed to have the day off. Obviously, to shop with David.

Cynthia disappeared into the breakroom without a word. *I hope she leaves without stopping to talk.* Traci fought to keep her emotions under control.

For the next two hours, a steady stream of customers visited the store, most of them young men who gravitated toward her. It was as if she had a sign hanging from her neck that read, "Make me more miserable."

After each customer, her eyes drifted toward the breakroom. The lump in her throat grew larger each time the door opened. David had chosen her best friend. How could she work with the woman now?

Ring-a-ling

The bell on the shop door sounded. Oh no! A guy in a Santa suit, plus what looked like a new Stetson and boots. St. Nick must have stopped at Cavender's Western Wear. She pasted the smile on her face.

Once inside the doorway, Santa stopped. His gaze swept the employees and zeroed in on Traci. She turned away. If he handed her a candy cane, she'd gag.

Cynthia appeared from the breakroom and made a beeline toward Santa. She led the man to the other side of the room as Traci glared at them. *I guess I should be thankful my two friends were happy.* The scene at the mall between David and Cynthia flashed through her mind. She left the counter and rushed to the restroom. How would she get through this day?

In the ladies' room, she snatched paper towels from the wall receptacle and ran cold water onto a fistful. She squeezed them until they were damp and pressed the sheets to her hot cheeks. Had anyone noticed her red face?

Several minutes later, she left the restroom, crossed the breakroom, and peeked from the door into the showroom. Santa nodded as Cynthia held a ring between her fingers. She finished the transaction and handed him a gold bag with the store's name emblazoned on it. The man hurried out to join the mob of shoppers.

Another fortunate woman would be getting a special gift for Christmas.

Monday morning came too soon as far as Traci was concerned. She hadn't heard from David that weekend until late Sunday night. He'd claimed to have worked two double shifts and slept in between. She cinched her mouth. No wonder he took the new job.

He'd never invited her to his apartment. Had Cynthia visited him? Why hadn't either of them mentioned their relationship?

Traci left for work, skipping another breakfast. As she drove, a familiar tune came from her purse. She pulled into a parking space outside the mall and grabbed the cell. "Hi, David."

"Hi. I'm at the airport to catch my flight. Sorry I didn't get to see you this weekend. You've been such a good friend, but I—"

Friend? In the background, a disembodied voice announced a flight. Her shoulders sagged.

"My flight is boarding now. I've gotta go. I've so much to talk over with you, but it'll have to wait. Bye."

"Goodbye. I wish—" *He hung up.* She hadn't given him his farewell gift, the new Bible the bookstore rushed to engrave with his name. His was so tattered. He'd obviously spent a lot of time reading it. Such a good man. Her heart sank. She hoped a great deal of prayer had gone into his decision to marry Cynthia. Not a good match, in her opinion. Traci's lips puckered.

She trudged through the mall toward the jewelry store. How could she work beside Cynthia each day?

As Traci stepped into the shop, a male employee cleaned a glass case in the window. Angela stood behind the counter. Traci headed to the back room, where she hung up her coat and filled her coffee cup. *No Cynthia*. Cup in hand, she peeked into the bathroom. Not there either.

She downed two swallows of coffee, placed the cup in the sink, and slipped into the showroom. "Angela, where's Cynthia?"

"Oh, haven't you heard? She requested a few days off. That's why I'm here on what should have been *my* day off. Something about her mother." Angela sashayed to her station.

Didn't need to be a mathematician to put two and two together. Cynthia's mother lived in New York. *And they hadn't bothered to tell me anything.* At least she'd have a *Cynthia-free* day. Sarcasm. She had to get her emotions under control.

The next morning, Traci awoke to another soaked pillow, a sledgehammer pounding in her head, and her kitten curled up in a ball behind her neck. "Good morning, Muffy." She pulled the kitten into her arms. The gentle sound of a tiny motor running at full blast warmed her heart.

She got out of bed, shuffled to the bathroom, and studied her face in the mirror. Puffy eyes in a pale face looked back. She couldn't go to work this way.

She picked up her cell and dialed her boss's number.

"I'm sorry to let you down, but I'm sick."

"I'm not surprised. Lots of viruses going around. Call me later and let me know if you think you'll be in tomorrow. You take care and get some rest."

Traci hung up and settled in bed with Muffy curled beside her.

Later that evening, her cell chimed out David's assigned tune. No way would she accept a *Dear Traci* phone call from New York. If he didn't think enough of her to tell her in person that he'd chosen Cynthia instead of her, she didn't want to talk to him now. She dismissed the call.

After four rejected calls and a text from him asking her to phone him, she huffed when a different tone rang. *Cynthia!* "Well, she wouldn't be told by her rival, either."

Though she returned to work on Wednesday, Traci's headache continued, along with her shattered heart. Before she left for the day, two more calls came in from David.

Should just block him. But perhaps she'd be able to endure hearing his good news later that night. *Maybe.*

Traci's cell vibrated on the nightstand. She rolled over in bed and checked the screen. Thursday, and David still kept trying to reach her. She rejected the call. "Take a hint." You'd think he would've gotten the message yesterday when he called the store, and she had Angela tell him she was busy.

She sat up in bed and stroked Muffy's soft, warm fur. Last night's dream broke her heart as David repeated wedding vows to Cynthia. "Why, God? Why did You let me fall in love with him?"

Traci laid back on the pillow, rolled to her side, and pulled the kitten to her. Another headache, and she'd wager her eyes were swollen too. She must have cried through the night. But she couldn't miss work again. She'd tell everyone she was coming down with a cold.

After dressing for work, she stood in the kitchen and eyed the refrigerator. She pursed her lips. Nothing enticed her. A scone from the coffee shop and a latte when she got to the mall would do.

Twenty minutes later, white paper bag in her left hand, tall vanilla latte in her right, she marched into the jewelry store and headed for the breakroom.

As Traci entered the room, Angela cut short her conversation with another employee who left. "Traci. I got a call from Cynthia this morning asking if you were okay. She said she called you several times but got voicemail."

"That's odd. Haven't received any." She slumped into a chair at the corner table. Now she'd become a liar.

Angela tilted her head. "Your eyes are puffy. Have you been crying?"

"No! Sorry for snapping. I don't feel well. The start of a cold, I guess."

"Oh." Angela backed away from her. "Try not to get sick. I've done enough covering for everyone." She poured the dregs of her coffee into the sink and tossed the paper cup in the trash. "See you out there. Today should be easy, now that we're past Black Friday." She stepped into the showroom.

Traci took a gulp of her latte, threw the rest in the trash along with her scone, and plodded out to her station to start the workday.

Only two customers filtered in during the morning hours. It had to be lunchtime by now. She glanced at the wall clock. Only eleven.

Ring-a-ling.

A man wearing a Santa suit, Stetson, and cowboy boots entered the store. *Not another one.* Was this the same guy from Black Friday? If he was, maybe he decided he didn't like the ring Cynthia showed him. She'd let Angela take care of him.

As he took a step toward her, Traci's eyes widened. *Don't want to deal with this one.* She dashed into the breakroom and poured a cup of coffee but wound up pouring it into the sink. Nothing tasted right.

When she returned to the showroom, Santa leaned against the counter right outside the door, his back to her. He turned before she could escape. "Traci Winterhaven?"

She froze in her tracks and spun to face him. *That can't be David's voice.* His chocolate brown eyes. "How do you know my name?" She scanned the room. Everyone stared at her.

The well-built Santa strode to the end of the display case and slipped around to the back.

A chill ran through her. "Customers aren't allowed behind the showcases." *Why didn't someone stop him?*

She opened her mouth to summon the male employee across the room but stopped when Santa lowered himself to one knee, removing his cowboy hat. Dark wavy hair framed his face. "David?"

He held up a small black box and opened it to reveal the iridescent marquise diamond ring she'd dreamed of having on her own finger one day.

"Will you marry me, Traci?"

"What?" *What was happening?* Her jaw dropped. She shook her head.

With his free hand, Santa caught the fluffy white beard and pulled it down to uncover his face.

Her lashes shot upward. *"David."*

He smiled. "Do I get an answer?"

Her mind whirled. Flashes of light blurred her vision. The room spun.

When Traci opened her eyes, David knelt on one side of her, minus the Santa coat and beard, pressing a cold paper towel to her cheeks. Cynthia stood on the other side. The redhead's brows furrowed as she bent and nudged a cup of water toward Traci. He supported her as she sat upright.

She took a sip. "What happened? I thought I saw—then there was Santa—hey! Why didn't you two tell me?" She glowered at Cynthia. "I thought I was your best friend."

"Tell you what?" Cynthia glanced at David, at the other employees leaning over the showcase from the customer side, and then at Traci. "Are you okay? You gave us a fright. I walked through the door and saw you plunge to the floor."

David drew in a deep breath. "You scared me to death, Traci. I thought you'd be surprised at my proposal, but I never expected you to faint dead away."

Once again, her mouth fell open. "Proposal? You asked Cynthia to marry you right here, with *that* ring, and neither of you even told me you were seeing—"

"Ask who? Cynthia?" His own jaw lowered.

He pulled Traci to her feet while Cynthia quirked her mouth and laid her hand on Traci's forehead. "Are you feverish? Why would he propose to me? He's like my little brother." She laughed. "Besides, he—"

"But, I saw you two outside McConnor's Grill at lunchtime on Black Friday."

Cynthia glanced at David and giggled. "The hug? Oh, no." She jerked her head back to Traci. "You thought—girl, that was a thank-you hug for showing him the ring you've ogled during the entire time you've worked here." She laughed so hard tears fell from her eyes.

Heat flooded Traci's cheeks. She bit her lip.

"Honey, did you not hear anything I said to you before you passed out? Don't you know how much I love you?" He quirked his mouth. "I'd better brush up on my romantic skills." He wrapped Traci in his arms and chuckled.

"I planned to wait until Christmas to propose. But when you didn't answer any of my calls after I left for New York, and you wouldn't come to the phone when I called the store, I worried. I even called Cynthia. Nothing made sense."

Cynthia stopped laughing and handed Traci the cupful of water. "I figured something was wrong when David said you didn't answer. Then I didn't get through either. That's why I came in."

Traci's stomach churned as she focused on Cynthia. "You came all the way from New York? Angela said you asked for days off because of your mom."

"New York? Nooo—oh, I guess I forgot to tell you. Mom moved to Houston last week. I took off to help her settle in and celebrate her fiftieth birthday."

Traci turned to David. "But you came back from New York?"

"I did. I didn't know what to think."

"Oh, David. I'm so sorry. I've made a lot of assumptions and a fool of myself."

His warm lips kissed her forehead. He wrapped his muscular arms around her once more and whispered, "It's okay." Then he knelt and held out the little black box. "Now...to repeat my question. Traci Winterhaven, will you—"

"Wait! One more thing."

He lowered the box and rose from the floor. His shoulders drooped.

"Why are you dressed as Santa? I was petrified when you came around the counter like a robber."

Cynthia burst out in giggles. "I told him it was a crazy idea. He tried out the costume the day he came in to pick up the ring. He was hoping you wouldn't recognize him so he could surprise you when he proposed."

David stifled a laugh. "And you didn't know it was me in my new hat and boots." He shrugged. "Surprise."

Traci blinked at him with her mouth open.

He lifted her jaw with his index finger. The mirth left his face. "Since I was coming in to see what was wrong, I decided to wear the costume as a joke. Then I thought I'd go ahead and propose, if you'd have me. Bad idea...the costume, I mean."

He gave her a Cheshire-cat grin and cupped her face in his hands. "I don't want to leave you behind ever again. I love you. I want to spend my first Christmas in New York with you—as my wife."

The warmth of his deep, chocolate brown eyes made her heart melt. "You mean, you aren't—I mean, you want—I mean—*yes*, I'll marry you." She threw her arms around his neck.

Customers and employees burst into applause as David's lips covered hers. He lifted her into his embrace.

No other kiss was ever so sweet. Just as she imagined it would be. A tingle ran through her all the way to her toes.

When their lips parted, he put on his Stetson and whispered in her ear. "Merry Christmas, little lady."

She nuzzled his neck.

Ring-a-ling

Traci glanced at the door, but no one had entered the store.

A wish granted? She smiled. *Thank You, Lord.*

The End

He that answereth a matter before he heareth it, it is folly and shame unto him. Proverbs 18:13

Trouble
With
Golden
Arrows

Trouble with Golden Arrows

Original Work: "The Trouble with Love and Golden Arrows"
First Place Winner of the CyFair Writers Valentine Short Story Contest, 2017

Genre: Fantasy

Eros has pulled one too many pranks in Mount Olympus, and his father Zeus has renamed him Cupid, ordering him to never mess with anyone's emotions again. Cupid has run away to the mortal world to continue his fun. When he comes upon a group of humans, he initiates his plans. But will they go as expected?

Trouble with Golden Arrows

Cupid crouched and peered over a balcony rail. Hmm, *Romeo and Juliet*, huh? He scanned the cast assembled to rehearse their first scene. Who would amuse him the most? The immortal pondered each face as the men and women muttered over their parts. No one suited his purpose. Too focused, too serious, too into themselves. But he'd have to pick someone, or two.

Life had been so boring since his name had been changed from Eros to Cupid by his father, Zeus. All because Dad was jealous. Cupid snickered. Could he help it if women found his handsome elf-like features more irresistible than his father's stormy appearance? Cupid ground his teeth. He'd show Zeus his restrictions meant nothing.

"Tell *me* what I can't do, will you?" he whispered in the balcony's darkness.

When the golden arrow made his brother Apollo fall in love with Daphne, and the toxic lead arrow caused her to be repulsed at the sight of him, Zeus had become furious. Cupid chuckled. A stroke of pure genius. Too bad Zeus had no sense of humor. "And then, to give me such a stupid name...Cupid? Apollo always had been Dad's favorite son."

As the golden-haired immortal leaned back against the balcony wall, he ruminated. His plan needed the right person.

"Forbid *me* from having fun with my spells, will you, Father?" He'd show Zeus how much he cared about his commands.

Mia stepped out onto the balcony platform of the makeshift castle in her elaborate costume as Juliet. She leaned over the ivy and rose-covered plywood railing constructed to appear as stone and smiled.

She stretched her arm, covered by the red velveteen sleeve of her gown, toward Romeo. Her heart did flip-flops as she lost herself in the deep blue of Luke's eyes. Her pulse raced as if she'd run a marathon instead of climbed the metal stairs behind the set.

Luke would recite his part without a hitch, as usual. If only she could deliver her lines and not stumble over them. She bit her bottom lip as butterflies took flight in her stomach.

Her feelings for him had grown stronger in the past several weeks—ever since Mr. Albright cast them in the leads. She'd hardly noticed him before he joined their theatrical group. But how her emotions had overwhelmed her during their scenes. Was it simply the story and parts they played or had she truly fallen in love for the first time in her life?

Luke wasn't like the guys who sought after her. He wasn't pushy or full of himself. He'd paid little attention to her aside from their performance.

Mia's cue called her thoughts to the present. She fought to control her quivering voice.

"Oh, Romeo, Romeo! Wherefore art thou, Romeo? Deny thy father and refuse thy name. Or, if thou wilt not, be but sworn my love, and I'll no longer be a Capulet."

The added bit of Shakespearean drama she managed to dredge up should make the director happy. Or would she lose the part to another female? Not at this late date. The play opened next weekend.

As they continued, Mia focused on the brown plumed hat Luke wore instead of the pools of his gorgeous blue eyes. So far, Mr. Albright hadn't interrupted them. He must think they were doing a good job.

Luke reached for her hand and caught Mia's gaze.

She froze. Her heart pounded. The romantic words were only spoken for the play. *Stop imagining he meant them for me.*

At the end of rehearsal, Mr. Albright strode onstage with a grin. His eyes roamed over the cast and found Mia. "You played Juliet as though you were the damsel herself." Murmurs broke out among the rest of the crew. "And you, Luke..."

Heat flooded Mia's cheeks. Had everyone guessed her feelings for Luke? If only she could melt into the upholstered chair she occupied.

Mr. Albright waved his arms and quieted the group. "Actors, you did a wonderful job tonight. We're ready for next weekend's performance. One more dress rehearsal Friday night."

The cast's chatter flowed across the auditorium as they followed Mia out the double doors and into the hall. She scampered toward her baby blue Mustang in the parking lot as fast as her legs would carry her. *Please don't let anyone stop me and mention Luke.*

"Hey, Mia. Slow down. I need to talk to you."

Oh no! Luke. She couldn't face him. Not now.

Cupid materialized in a clump of trees between the auditorium and parking lot. He watched as the dark-haired young man who played Romeo dashed out the building and hurried to catch his Juliet. Cupid's eyes drifted to the young woman with long, wavy light-blonde hair. Her face turned a beautiful shade of rose as Romeo spoke to her. Nice!

Those two would be his first victims. Obviously attracted to one another. But he wouldn't give them a big dose of infatuation to cause them to sweat and fumble their speech and act like lovesick fools. They'd already reached that stage.

He shook his head. Nah. With such magnetism already in play, he could make better use of their emotions later. Over the weekend, during the play. What a gas it'd be. One shot to each of them with a pure gold arrow, and they'd act out their passions to the extreme in front of everyone.

Wait. That wouldn't be enough enjoyment. Not the fun he sought. The old lovey-dovey stuff was too boring. He'd rather stir up trouble between two lovers.

Hmm. What do we have here?

The young man who played Benvolio in the production strode out the doors. "Hey, Luke! Hold up. Let's grab a hamburger."

Romeo waved and left Juliet standing next to her car. She shrugged, got in, and drove out of the parking spot. Cupid's eyebrows rose.

As Romeo glanced back at the Mustang, he rubbed the back of his neck and sighed.

He'd fallen hard for his Juliet. Cupid snickered. This would offer days of amusement.

The second man stopped beside Romeo and followed his line of vision to Juliet's retreating car. "Luke, how many times do I have to tell you, you'll get nowhere with Mia if you don't make a move?"

Romeo pressed his lips together and winced. "When I'm around her, I can't find the right words, I can't breathe. I wanted to ask her to dinner tonight, but when I gazed into those crystal green eyes, I stammered."

"Ha! That's a laugh." Benvolio faced Romeo. "You, Luke? The modern-day Robert Burns—who spews Shakespeare out of your mouth like a waterfall? Man, you could even play Juliet's part and make it believable."

After a punch to Benvolio's arm, Romeo walked off. "Shut up, Owen. I already feel stupid enough."

Benvolio's eyes returned to the blue Mustang as it turned onto the street. A gust of wind blew a thick lock of Juliet's hair out the window.

Now was the time. Cupid raised his bow and shot an enchanted golden arrow through Benvolio's back into his heart. The young man froze, rigid as an ice sculpture. His eyes rounded and glued to Juliet's blonde mane waving at him. His jaw dropped.

Cupid cackled and imagined red hearts popping out of the man's chest like the cartoon characters on Saturday morning television. A Cheshire cat grin spread across the immortal's handsome face. He'd wait for Benvolio to find Juliet at Friday night's rehearsal. Cupid doubled over with laughter. Then he'd complete his plan. *This'll be good.*

With a snap of his fingers, he vanished.

On Friday night, Owen arrived early at the hall to catch Mia before rehearsal. He had to tell her how he felt. Luke had dragged his feet long enough. If he was going to lose the goddess to someone, it might as well be his best friend.

Owen seated himself on the bench outside the building's entrance and waited for his new heartthrob to arrive. A loud crash in the street to the right caught his attention. Just a fender-bender, but those two drivers were really getting into it. Not his problem.

When he turned to the parking lot at his left, Mia's Mustang sat in the front row. He stared at the tinted windshield and watched for the driver's door to open. *Come on, Mia.* Maybe she didn't realize it was so late. Rehearsal would start soon.

He stood and ran to her car. Empty? How had he missed her? The accident. She must've parked and hurried into the building during the drivers' scuffle.

Owen sprinted to the entrance. He'd catch her before she reached the dressing room.

As he entered the building, he scanned the hallway and then peered at his watch. Costume time. Boy, she was fast.

His heart heavy, Owen trudged to the men's dressing room. What had happened to him? He'd never been interested in Mia. She wasn't his type. What was wrong with him? If Chloe found out he was chasing after Mia, she'd kill him. He'd been dating his little redhead for two years. No doubt she expected him to propose soon, and he'd been seriously thinking about it too. She'd drill him full of those needles she used to repair the costumes if she caught him lusting after her friend.

As he changed, Owen's thoughts turned to his best friend. When Luke found out, he'd hate him. They'd been friends since college. But not after tonight. What was he doing, risking their friendship?

Cupid popped into the balcony to observe the dress rehearsal. It seemed an eternity after the curtain rose. A frown spread across his face. Would the time never be right?

At the start of scene two, Benvolio stood in the wings, eyes fixed on Juliet. Romeo began his romantic speech, and lovesick Benvolio glared at him.

Too perfect. Cupid snickered again. He couldn't have planned it better. Now he'd wait until she looked Benvolio's way.

Juliet hesitated with her next line. Her eyebrows knit, and she glanced at the line prompter. Benvolio stood where the screen should have been.

A golden arrow rested between Cupid's fingers, the bowstring taut. He let it fly at Juliet and backed away from the railing, dancing a jig. She'd fall in love with Benvolio, and Romeo would hate his friend, thinking he'd betrayed him.

Minutes later, Cupid peeked over the railing. His grin slid to a frown. Juliet gazed love-struck at Romeo. *What happened?* The golden arrow had hit her while she was staring in Benvolio's direction. This wasn't supposed to happen.

Cupid slammed his bow and quiver to the floor. The stage manager glanced upward toward the balcony. The immortal jumped back into the shadows and then glared at the golden arrows. *How had things gone so wrong?* He had it all figured out. Something wasn't right here.

From the far end of the balcony, Cupid glowered over the rail at Romeo and Juliet, who spoke their lines to perfection as if they meant every word. Benvolio stood in the wing, but he no longer paid attention to Romeo or Juliet. His muscular arm circled another female who held a magnificent regal purple gown draped over her shoulder. She stuck a needle into the pincushion attached to her wrist and smiled up at Benvolio.

As Cupid grimaced, Benvolio leaned in and covered the woman's mouth with his own. Their lips parted, and she threw her arms around his neck.

"No." They couldn't be in love now, not after the arrow pierced Benvolio as he ogled Juliet. "My spells have never gone wrong before."

In disgust, the golden-haired immortal turned and slid down the inside of the balcony railing to the floor. He narrowed his eyes. His lips drew into a taut line, and a hiss of fury escaped. "Someone messed with my spell," he spewed between clenched teeth.

"Now, who might that be?" The all-too-familiar, powerful, authoritarian voice echoed in Cupid's head.

Zeus. How had he found him?

Like rolling thunder, Zeus's voice roared. "Didn't I warn you tampering with the emotions of others would lead to your downfall?"

Cupid jumped to his feet with a scowl. His brows lowered as he took one last glimpse of the two enraptured couples on stage.

The sound of lightning crashed through the sky as Zeus laughed. "I've canceled your spells. You've been under surveillance, my son. If you had enhanced the affections these mortals possessed, I'd have forgiven your defiance." His voice became more menacing. "This time, you went too far. You need a lesson that will stick."

While the actors went on with their roles in *Romeo and Juliet*, an angry Zeus plucked Cupid out of the mortals' world by his ear and transported his son back to Mount Olympus.

Cupid sulked. *Why hadn't I listened?* Now he had to spend the rest of his days in hiding. What an underhanded trick to play on an innocent, fun-loving son. Zeus had no business ordering Aphrodite to give Athena a dose of the love potion.

Although...having a lovely creature like Athena catch him wouldn't have been such a bad idea if it weren't for one problem, *my wife, Psyche.*

Zeus had been so angry at him, he'd told Psyche that the beautiful goddess Athena had been shot with a golden arrow while she welcomed Cupid home. Everyone knew who used gold arrows. *Me. But I didn't shoot her.* His father cast his own spell to do the dirty work.

"Oh, no! There's Psyche again. And this time, she's with Cyclops, who's carrying a fist-full of Zeus's thunderbolts. If he lets loose with one of those—I'm doomed!" *Why didn't I listen to my father?*

The End

Honour thy father and thy mother: that thy days may be long upon the land which the LORD thy God giveth thee. Exodus 20:12

It Happened
on the Bayou

It Happened on the Bayou

Genre: Romance

Four years ago, Brianna left her fiancé at the altar without explanation. After realizing she'd never stopped loving him, she's come home to apologize. Will he forgive her? Is there still a future for them...or has he moved on?

It Happened on the Bayou

Brianna O'Sullivan pushed open the wooden gate between her parents' backyard and the bayou right-of-way. It creaked shut. She caught the wind-blown strands of her long blonde hair and tucked them behind her ears as she strolled the broad grassy path to the slope descending to the water. Unopened bluebonnets dotted the area as the swollen stream gurgled over rocks below. In their youth, she and Connor McLaughlin had spent hours sitting on this bank, dreaming and making plans for the future.

Why had she called him? Of all the foolhardy ideas. What would she say to him after so many years of silence? He'd agreed to see her out of politeness, no doubt.

Brianna sat at the edge of the slope. How humiliated he must have been when she left. Only her parents knew where she'd gone. And she'd sworn them to secrecy.

A red Chevy Impala pulled into the utility building parking lot on the opposite side of the ravine. It backed into a space near the footbridge over the bayou. Connor emerged with a grin on his face and strode across the bridge toward her as if the last four years hadn't happened. His dark brown hair tousled in the strong breeze.

Maybe he didn't hate her. For the life of her, she couldn't fathom why not. Her mind envisioned how the scene must have been. Connor dressed in a tuxedo at the front of the church as he read the goodbye note she'd asked an usher to give him right before the ceremony began. She'd already taken a cab to the airport. An expression of unbelief covered his face. She still hadn't forgiven herself for hurting him. But had he forgiven her?

He climbed up the slope and sat beside her on the grass. "Brianna. Pretty as ever. I'm glad you're home."

"Are you?" Her brows pinched. Although the late February afternoon sun warmed her, her lower lip quivered. "I wasn't certain you'd ever want to see me again."

Connor crossed his legs and leaned back on his palms. "In all honesty, I wasn't either. When I got your message...well...we've grown up."

Brianna gazed into the emerald green eyes that won her heart seven years earlier at the beginning of their senior year in high school. Up until then, they'd simply been good friends. What a quarterback he'd been. After months of dating, Connor had admitted her "baby-blues" had the same effect on him. From puppy to true love.

He turned to the water, silent. What were his thoughts?

She followed his line of vision and returned to her memories.

After graduation, Connor had proposed, and they were to be married in September two years later. Over two hundred people were invited to her parents' home for the backyard ceremony in front of the massive waterfall her dad had built.

A great egret gracefully landed on the edge of the swollen stream below them and brought her attention to the present. Recent storms had caused the bayou to rise above normal. The elegant white bird stretched its neck and then began a search for food along the side of the stream. This spot had been special to her and Connor since they were preteens. The ceremony would have been beautiful with birds in and out throughout the reception. She should have planned the wedding for the following March when the egrets displayed their full mating plumage.

Her face wilted, and her eyebrows furrowed. If only they'd listened to his parents and waited another year or two. Perhaps she wouldn't have panicked on their wedding day. What a fool she'd been. Connor had everything going for him. Planned on a great career as an architect. He was perfect. But that was what scared her.

"Penny for your thoughts." Connor smiled at her.

"Just wondering."

"About?"

"Why I left you."

"It's in the past." Connor rose from the grass and held his hand out to her. "What do you say we grab some coffee? You can tell me what's happened to you in the last four years away from Houston."

Brianna stared at him. Didn't he care why she left? She'd never explained to anyone, not even her parents, and they hadn't wanted to upset her more than she already was that day. They never brought it up later, either. But then, Mom and Dad had always accepted her decisions without question. *"Make sure you've thought it out and prayed about it," they'd say.*

Connor pulled her up, and they brushed the blades of dead grass from their jeans. She peered up at him from her bent position. His teeth rested on his lower lip. "What?" She straightened. Was he hesitant to tell her something? She peeked at his left hand—no wedding ring. Brianna breathed out a relieved sigh. *What did he hold back?*

After an uncomfortably quiet fifteen-minute ride, they arrived at the Coffee Bean Café. Brianna ordered a café mocha, then eyed the interior. Same old place. Coffee colored walls displaying pictures of cups and mugs in every size, shape, and color. With a grin, she eyed Connor. "Bet yours'll be hazelnut espresso."

The right side of Connor's mouth curved upward. "Still my favorite."

But was she? The ride to the coffee shop had been uncomfortably quiet.

While they waited for the barista to call Connor's name, they found a small table near the rear of the room where a conversation would be easier. Brianna faced the front of the shop. "Not many customers."

Connor took the seat facing her, then shifted to do his own quick survey. "Saturday afternoon. People have to get errands done if they work during the week. A lull in the action." He lifted his brows, shrugged, and turned back.

Several minutes later, the barista called out, "Hazelnut espresso and café mocha for Connor." He set their order on the counter and greeted another customer as he entered the café. "Welcome to the Coffee Bean."

Connor picked up their drinks and placed the cup of mocha in front of her.

Brianna took a sip and closed her eyes. "Mmm. No one makes café mocha like this place."

"I knew you'd say that." He chuckled, but the mirth never reached his eyes.

What was wrong? She wrapped her fingers around his on the Styrofoam cup. "My turn. Penny for *your* thoughts."

He narrowed his eyes as if he weighed a decision. Then he pursed his lips and gave a slight shake of the head. "Do you remember the day I rescued you from the bayou?" Connor drew the cup closer to him. Brianna's nails hit the table.

"How could I forget? I almost drowned. The water was even higher than this spring. If you hadn't run by when I slipped and tumbled in—" She shook her head.

The experience had never left her mind for long. The stream swollen from spring rains, the current so swift. She'd floundered until a hand clutched hers. He'd appeared out of nowhere and dragged her to the bank.

"I'd have been a goner." She leaned toward him over the table. "If I hadn't already been in love with you—" She laughed.

"It was a miracle I was there."

"I'll forever be grateful you were." Her heart throbbed. "And I'm so glad you're here now."

Sadness drifted over Connor's face. His jaw muscles twitched as he sat up straight. His eyes riveted to hers. "Brianna, didn't your parents tell you?"

"Tell me what?"

"Maybe not. But before you hear it from someone else, I have to."

She froze. "What?"

"I'm seeing someone."

Her stomach tightened as if in a vise. She shouldn't be surprised. A handsome man like Connor had always attracted the interest of women. She'd disappeared from his life and dismissed his every call. It had been wrong of her, but she couldn't face him after what she'd done. Not even from a thousand miles away. Her heart and body ached.

Whenever she'd called her parents, they never mentioned old friends, especially not Connor. And they only said he was fine when she asked.

Brianna tried to raise a smile. "I'm not surprised. Who is she?"

"Jessica."

A rock landed in Brianna's heart.

Jessica? "My bridesmaid at our—*that* Jessica?" The black-haired nymph had her eye on Connor all through high school. She said he was perfect. And the woman he married had to be flawless. Anyone less than that would fail him.

Briana knew she was far from perfect. Jessica obviously thought she was? Heat trailed up Brianna's neck.

"How long have you been with her? Are you engaged?"

A few weeks later, Brianna took on every task she could find to keep herself busy at her new secretarial job in the local hospital. The busier, the better. Less time to dwell on her past mistakes. *Move on with life. Everything's fine.* Who was she kidding? Things would never be fine as long as Connor was with Jessica. Brianna rubbed her tense forehead. She'd made a colossal blunder. Now she paid for it with a broken heart.

As Brianna slid into the driver's seat of her silver Chevy on the way to lunch, her cell rang. She looked at the screen but didn't recognize the number. "Hello?"

"Brianna? This is Amy Patterson."

"Amy? Hi. I meant to catch up with you after church last Sunday."

"Connor told me you found a job here in the hospital. Your mom gave me your cell number. I work on the fourth floor."

The corners of Brianna's mouth turned up. Same old exuberant Amy.

"When I dropped by your office, your boss said you'd left ten minutes ago. Thought we might meet for lunch."

Brianna's heart eased. Amy had always lifted her spirits. "I'd love to. My plan was to have lunch at a restaurant, but I'm in the parking lot, so I can meet you in the hospital cafeteria if you'd prefer."

"Yeah. That'll give us more time to talk. See you in a few."

Brianna ended the call and tossed the phone into her purse. She hopped out of the car and headed into the building.

When she entered the lunchroom, Amy waved to her from a spot next to a window. The redhead's cherub-like face lit up. Brianna hastened to her, and they hugged. "I'm so glad you called, Amy. Let's get our food."

In the cafeteria line, Brianna grabbed a salad and a carton of milk while Amy opted for a hamburger and fries. They paid for their meal and hurried back to the table.

While she munched her greens, Brianna studied Amy. "You haven't changed one bit since high school. What've you been up to these past four years?"

With a wide grin, Amy lifted her left hand and flashed a wedding ring.

Brianna's heart sank. "Well. Congratulations. You and Bill, huh?"

"Yes. We were hitched last year. Wish you'd been here. I would've asked you to be my Maid of Honor. But then you'd of had to be a

Matron of Honor, cuz you and—oh, I'm sorry. I shouldn't have brought it up." She winced.

Brianna patted Amy's hand and forced a smile. "It's okay."

Amy's brows lowered. "So you aren't angry that Jessica finally got her hooks into your man?"

"Connor's free to see whomever he chooses."

"But *Jessica*? She tried to get his attention in high school and continued even when you and Connor were engaged. She's still at it. After you left, she made a big play for Connor, to *comfort* him. Wherever he went, she'd show up."

"How do you know?"

Amy took a bite of her burger, chewed, and swallowed. "Heard it from her own lips. Don't get me wrong. We're not friends by any stretch of the word, but she's always, let's say, flaunted her successes to anyone within ears' reach."

"Connor has a mind of his own. He chose Jessica."

Amy sat erect. She lowered her right brow and raised the left. Her mouth pulled to the right side. "While he pined away for you."

"Not likely after four years. They're together now, even if they aren't engaged yet."

"This isn't a recent event." Amy cleared her throat. "They started to date soon after you left. Brianna, wake up. I saw how Connor watched you at church. He has deep feelings for you, not her. And if he's so into her, why doesn't she have a ring on her finger after *four years*?"

While she drove home from work, Amy's words replayed in Brianna's mind. Could it be true? That Connor still loved her? Should she try to win him back? But if he wanted to see her, he'd have called. She'd given him her number. He and Jessica weren't engaged. And he had her parents' phone number. She'd give anything to believe he hadn't gotten over her.

Brianna parked her car in the driveway behind her old home. She really should get a place of her own now that she'd returned to Houston, but she dreaded the loneliness that led to memories of what might have been.

Tears filled her eyes as she strolled out the backyard gate and dropped to the grass along the bayou. She stared at the turbulent water. Even if he still loved her, how could he forgive her? She hadn't forgiven herself. So many times, she'd wanted to come home but couldn't face him.

It had taken her new boyfriend's words while in Kentucky to open her eyes. *"You're not in love with me."* His voice silently echoed. *"You're in love with someone else. And your heart's bound up so tight with his, there's no room for me."*

He was right. Every time she had gazed into Kurt's green eyes, she saw Connor's.

But if Connor loved her, why did he act indifferent whenever they ran into each other? Self-defense? No doubt, he thought she'd hurt him again.

Should she call and ask if they could talk? She sighed. Talk about what? His feelings toward her or hers for him? A thought came to mind. *The teen group at church.* She'd ask his opinion about working with them. He'd always given her advice in the past. "Then I'll work the conversation around to us."

Brianna raced into the house, grabbed her purse, and fished out her cell. She pressed Connor's number but disconnected before it rang. The phone clunked onto the coffee table, and she sighed again. She stepped into the bathroom to splash cool water on her hot cheeks. *You're a coward,* the voice in her head yelled. *Call him.*

She marched into the living room, picked up the cell, and punched in the number. As her finger poised to disconnect again, a strange voice answered.

"The White House. State your business." A chuckle followed.

Her eyes popped open so wide they hurt. "*What?*"

Laughter rang out in her ear. "I'm sorry. Couldn't resist. Connor's gonna kill me for this. Mike here, answering Connor's phone. He's not here, but I'll be happy to take a message."

"Mike?"

"Yeah, I'm his roommate. And you are?"

"Oh. This is Brianna. But why do you have Connor's cell phone?" She paced the length of the room.

"Aha! The infamous Brianna. I heard you're back."

She sucked in a deep breath. What had Connor told him? *Derail the subject.* "Why do you have his cell?"

"Yeah. Well, he's gone off without it this evening. Said he shouldn't be gone long. Can he return your call?"

"Ummm...sure."

"Your number?"

"He has it." And the phone recorded it when she called. *Nice try, Mike.*

"I'll bet he has. You know, you're the reason he's so gun-shy around women now. Ah...sorry. Out of line. But you sure messed the guy up."

She slumped to the couch. Was *that* what Connor had told everyone?

The following Sunday, Brianna took a seat on the opposite side of the sanctuary from Connor and Jessica. A tall, lanky man sat on the other side of him. *Must be the rude roommate.* Oh, who was she to judge? He'd voiced his opinion, which he was entitled to. But why hadn't he told Connor she'd called? Maybe he did, and Connor had no interest in talking to her.

Brianna refocused on the preacher's words.

"...and you know that means we've been shorthanded in the youth department. Yes, this is a call for volunteers, especially with the teens. If you're interested, please see me after the service."

As the congregation filed out of the sanctuary, Brianna approached him. "Pastor Gray, you said you needed help with the teens. I'd like to work with them."

"Yes, we do need help."

"May I volunteer?"

"You sure can. You always had a way with the younger set. We've been shorthanded since Connor quit. We'd love to have you."

Connor had worked with them? That would've been so awkward. She'd wager Jessica persuaded him to quit. She'd never cared for kids and always thought she was superior to anyone younger than her. "Do you have time to tell me about the work now?"

The pastor led her to his study. After he gave her a list of upcoming meetings, he handed her the year's schedule. "We'll see you Thursday evening."

Brianna shook his hand. "Thursday. Seven p.m."

Pastor Gray reseated himself behind his desk.

She stepped out of his office, turned, and collided with Connor's muscular chest. "Oh!"

As papers flew everywhere, Connor's arms encircled her. In a flash, he snatched his hands from her back and grasped her shoulders, as if to steady her. She gaped into his green eyes, and a tingle ran through her.

He released her. "Sorry. Should've watched where I was going." He bent to gather the scattered pages from the floor.

"No. It's my fault. I should have looked before I stepped into the hall." She picked up a few fly-aways from behind her. Heat flooded her face. His arms had felt so good.

When he stood and smiled at her, she bit her lip and handed him his papers. "These are yours."

He flipped through the stack in his hands and pulled out a couple. "And these must be yours." He grinned.

"Thanks. I called your cell last week. Your roommate answered."

Connor's brows pinched together. "He did?" He looked up at the ceiling. "Oh. It must have been the night I stepped out without it." He tilted his head. "He didn't tell me you phoned. I haven't checked for missed calls because there are so many from...robocalls. What'd he say?"

"Well...'The White House'...I think." She pursed her lips.

Her statement ignited a laugh. Connor nodded. "Yep, that's Mike. His last name is White, and he pulls the stunt on his phone all the time. Figures he'd take advantage of the opportunity on mine. Did you leave a message with him? He's not the forgetful type."

"I gave him my name. I don't think he likes me."

"Does he know you?"

"Apparently, he knows enough *about* me." She grimaced.

Connor sucked in his lower lip. "I'm sorry, Brianna. Mike's been my roommate since shortly after you left. He served as my sounding board back then. I said things I shouldn't have."

"I don't blame you."

"Just what did he say to you?" Connor frowned.

"It's not important."

"It is to me."

Her hand touched his forearm. "Let it go. It was a hard time for you, and it was my fault."

Connor shook his head. He covered her hand with his. "No. You had cold feet, that's all. And I let my anger get the best of me."

Brianna scanned the empty hall. "Everyone's gone. I'd better go too."

"Why were you in the pastor's study? Sorry, I shouldn't ask. It's none of my business."

"I volunteered to work with the youth group."

"No kidding. I was on my way to ask Pastor Gray for my old position with the teens." He laughed. "I guess they could still use another hand. You suppose?"

His smile sent a quiver of hope through her.

In the parking lot after evening service, Connor crossed his arms over his chest and glared at Jessica. "As a matter of fact, Brianna *has* volunteered. But it had nothing to do with my decision. I missed my time with the kids. Never should have let you talk me out of it." What had gotten into this woman?

Jessica glowered at him. "We don't spend enough time together as it is." She pinned her hands on her hips. "I saw you two in the hallway. Your arms around her." She turned and stomped off toward her car.

How had he let himself get involved with Jessica in the first place? Not only had he been forced to stop answering his phone, but every time he turned around, she was there. Had he been that blind from hurt and anger after Brianna left? Yes...he had. He'd let Jessica cool off, then he had to talk to her.

Connor pulled out his cell and called Brianna. Time to put the past in the past.

"Hello, Connor."

The melodic tone of her voice tugged at a string in his heart. Warmth surged through him. "Hi. Would you have dinner with me tomorrow night? I have things I need to say—to talk about."

"There's something I need to say to you too."

Brianna glanced at Connor while he drove her home after dinner, eyes fixed on the road ahead. What a disappointment. She'd planned to say so much to him, but nothing came out right. Everything she said had sounded contrived. She'd made excuses. How could she tell him how sorry she was or make up for the hurt she'd caused him? His eyes had changed from misty to hard through the evening. Did he regret asking her to dinner? Was Jessica aware Connor was with her?

He parked in the driveway and shut off the engine. As he turned to her, he laid his hand on her arm. Goosebumps ran to her shoulder. "Before you go in, take a stroll along the bayou with me. Our conversation tonight at dinner didn't come out as planned. I have more to tell you."

"Sure. The sunset is gorgeous. The birds should be ready to fly to the rookery. What a beautiful backdrop it would've made for the wed—" Her teeth clamped down on her lower lip. She'd done it again. No more sad wedding-day memories.

Her eyes focused on him. He pressed his lips together as he led her through the backyard gate.

From the other side of the ravine, a figure jogged down the grass, across the footbridge, and toward them. They'd have to wait to talk. She needed more privacy before she spoke the words that hung between them like an ugly curtain. She had to tell him how wrong she'd been to run out on him four years ago when all she had to do was tell him how scared she'd been.

When they reached the slope, Connor spun to face her. "Brianna. I have to say this. I've harbored these feelings ever since you ducked out on me."

She focused on his eyes. "You have every right to be angry. I'm so sorry for what I did. I can't begin to tell you how miserable I've been for the past four years because of my actions."

He touched her cheek. "It's all right. We were too young and—"

"We may have been young, but that doesn't excuse what I did. I should have talked to you. We should have taken your parents' advice and waited until we graduated from college." She reached up and covered his hand.

His other hand touched her neck. "When you left, my heart shattered. I walked around like a zombie until you came home."

"Oh, Connor." Tears flooded her eyes.

He drew nearer, and their lips touched.

Hands grabbed Brianna's shoulders from behind and shoved her down the slope toward the water. Her body careened through the grass and bluebonnets. Unable to stop the momentum, Brianna tumbled into the swollen stream. Cold, rushing water closed around her. As she tried to get a foothold, her ankle scraped against the rocky bottom. Stems from submerged plants scratched her legs as the swift current carried her along. She couldn't keep her feet on the bottom. Her head popped up again, and she sputtered. Once more, she slipped under the dark, swirling water.

Someone grasped her by the waist and pulled her to the bank. *Connor.*

He scooped her into his arms and ran to the house. As they burst in from the back porch, the door banged into a cabinet.

Mrs. O'Sullivan's eyes widened. "Brianna! What happened? Your leg's bloody. Connor, what happened?"

"She was pushed into the bayou."

Her mother's eyes grew round.

Connor shook his head. "It wasn't me."

With Brianna in his arms, he followed Mrs. O'Sullivan up the stairs and into the bathroom. As he placed Brianna on her feet, she shook. Her mother pushed him out into the hallway.

The door slammed shut.

Connor stared at the closed door. "I'll...be on the porch." Tears welled in his eyes as he hurried down the steps and out the back door. His heart raced. He dropped onto a patio chair at the far end and lowered his head into his hands. A puddle from his wet clothes formed beneath him, and he shivered. *Jessica!* What had gone through her mind? Brianna could have been badly injured on those rocks in the stream or even drowned in the swift current.

Heat surged into his neck, and he ground his teeth.

A few minutes later, Brianna's mother stepped onto the porch. Connor jumped from the chair. "Is she all right?"

Mrs. O'Sullivan nodded. She handed him a jacket. "Put this on before you get sick. It's my husband's fishing jacket, but it'll keep you warm. What happened? Brianna said she wasn't sure. Someone grabbed her from behind while she talked to you. The next moment, she was under water in the middle of the bayou. She said you lifted her out and carried her here."

Connor flipped the jacket over his shoulders. A hard knot tightened in his stomach. "I know who it was. I'll take care of it."

"Who?"

"Jessica Davis. I saw a jogger come toward us. Her hair must have been tucked up under the baseball cap, and she wore sunglasses. But I'm sure it was her."

"The girl you've been seeing since Brianna left?"

"Yes. But not anymore." He looked at Mrs. O'Sullivan and took a deep breath. "I've never gotten over Brianna. Jessica was a bandage for my wounds, nothing more. I realized it when Brianna returned. I'm still in love with your daughter."

The attractive silver-haired woman smiled with a twinkle in her blue eyes, so much like Brianna's. "Don't tell Brianna I said this, but she's not over you either. Whenever she wrote to me, or we'd talk, she'd ask if I'd seen you. I didn't have the heart to tell her about your new girlfriend."

"Ex-girlfriend." Connor rested his hand on Mrs. O'Sullivan's shoulder. "You're sure she'll be okay?"

"She's shaken up and might be sore tomorrow."

"And her leg?"

"Scraped the skin off. But she'll be fine. I've cleaned, applied salve, and wrapped it. She's taken a couple of aspirin."

He nodded and ran down the stairs. "Excuse me, I have to have a serious talk with someone. Please, tell Brianna I'll call later."

Connor pulled out of the O'Sullivans' driveway and raced toward Jessica's apartment building. She had a lot to answer for. And he had to end any relationship she thought they had.

Several minutes later, he flew up the steps to the third-floor apartment and banged on the door until it opened. "What did you think you were doing, Jessica? It's a miracle Brianna wasn't seriously injured."

"I didn't do anything. What are you talking about?"

"Cut the innocent act. When you flung Brianna down the bank of the bayou, I recognized you. I can't believe you did that."

"I still don't know what you're talking about." Jessica lifted her chin.

"Oh, yes, you do." How had he become involved with this...this? "You may as well own up to it."

She stepped into her apartment. Her lips pressed together, and tears came to her eyes. Jessica took in a big gulp of air and lowered her head. "Okay. I admit it was me."

Her head slowly rose. "I was angry. I didn't mean for her to wind up in the water. When I saw your arms around Brianna in the hall at church yesterday, I was hurt. Our relationship has gone nowhere. The more I pictured you two, the angrier I became. I decided to go to her house and confront her. Tell her how awful she'd treated you four years ago. This isn't fair. I lost it when I saw you kiss her at the bayou." She gazed at him with watery eyes. "I didn't mean to hurt her."

Connor's brows furrowed. Was it an act? Everything was always about her. He took Jessica's arm and led her out of her apartment to the balcony at the far end of the hall. "Sit down."

She lowered herself to the wrought iron bench and peered up at him, her cheeks wet with tears. She must be sincere. His anger subsided.

"Brianna has cuts and bruises, but she'll be all right." He sat in a matching chair facing her.

A tear slid over Jessica's cheek.

"Jessica, I owe you an apology. I didn't realize it until Brianna came home, but I've been stringing you along with no intention of going anywhere with this relationship. It was unfair of me. When Brianna left, I needed your attention. It's so clear now. But it was wrong. Forgive me."

"I—" Jessica ran to her apartment and slammed the door behind her.

Several months later, Brianna glanced at Connor as he drove them to dinner. She focused out the side window as the houses whizzed by. "Has Jessica spoken to you since I fell into the bayou?"

"Fell? I'd hardly say you fell. But no, she hasn't. She hasn't been to church either. I hope she's all right. But I don't want to check on her and give her the wrong idea. Have you heard anything from her?"

"No. The other day, Amy told me she's trying to talk Jessica into returning to church. This is all my fault. Do you think I should try to call her?"

"Why don't we give it a couple more weeks and see if Amy gets anywhere. It might be for the best."

Brianna nodded. "I suppose you're right. Jessica must hate me."

Connor slipped his hand over hers as he drove. "Nothing would have changed between Jessica and me, even if you hadn't come home. And nothing had happened between us for the entire four years. We dated, and I may have given her a peck on the mouth on occasion. But that was it. Even when she tried to get romantic, I didn't do or feel anything. I still loved you. Always have, always will."

And yet, our relationship hasn't moved forward in the last few months either. Why? Here it was September, and all they did was see each other on the weekends or talk on the phone. She deserved it after breaking his heart. Did he fear she'd leave him again?

Connor parked the car, and they strolled toward the Italian restaurant. The aroma of garlic and herbs filled the air. Once inside, the maître d' seated them at the far end of the room. Brianna gazed into the foyer as a very tall, blond-haired man entered. *Kurt?* What was he doing here?

Kurt strode up to her with a smile. "Brianna. Your mom told me where you'd gone for dinner." He reached his hand over to Connor. "Hi, I'm Kurt Weber. A...friend...of Brianna's from Kentucky. Sorry to intrude, but I couldn't wait to tell her I'm in town."

She glanced at Connor, whose brows pinched. He shook Kurt's hand. "Always nice to meet one of Brianna's friends." Connor's eyes sought hers, then returned to Kurt. "Why don't you join us?"

"Thanks, if you don't mind my barging in." He sat in the seat between her and Connor at the square, gingham-covered table. "Got a promotion, and I've been transferred to Houston. I thought you might show me around your home town, lady."

She forced a smile to her lips. "Congratulations on the promotion."

Though Kurt monopolized most of the conversation during dinner, Connor appeared to enjoy the ins and outs of hospital administration. She hadn't spoken two sentences since Kurt joined them, but she was relieved they were getting along. *Instant best buds, it seems.*

After dessert, Kurt paid for the meal. "Say, Brianna always talked about the good church she went to here in town? I'd like to visit."

Connor grinned as they walked out the door. He handed Kurt the directions to the church, and they shook hands again.

Kurt shoved the note in his pocket. "Okay then, I'll see you two tomorrow morning. Enjoy the rest of your evening." He winked at Brianna and strode off.

Tension mounted as Connor drove them to Brianna's home. "So...who is this Kurt?"

As Brianna waited for Connor to join her at church on Sunday, Kurt strutted up the aisle. He stopped at her pew. Why couldn't he have waited a couple of weeks to show up to allow Connor time to adjust?

"Good morning. Where's Connor? Mind if I sit with you?"

"Connor sits there."

Kurt slid his well-toned frame next to her. "I'll leave room for him."

Without a glimmer of joy on his face, Connor strode up behind Kurt. "Excuse me, you're in my seat."

Kurt stifled a chuckle and moved to the other side of Brianna.

Connor shot him a scathing glare and sat in the vacated spot.

She sighed. *Oh, boy.* This would be an interesting service. First, Jessica shows up, and now Kurt. At least Jessica sat on the far side of the auditorium. Those two should get together. Now that Connor knew Kurt had been her boyfriend in Kentucky, no more best buds. She gulped.

The tension lessened through the pastor's message until they started to leave. When she moved into the aisle, Kurt took Brianna's arm and put his mouth to her ear. "I need to talk to you...alone."

Connor's eyes narrowed. He did an about-face and stormed out of the sanctuary.

She pulled away from Kurt. "What about?"

"Us." He eased past her into the aisle.

"There is no us, Kurt. You were right. I'm still in love with Connor."

Kurt picked up her left hand. "I don't see an engagement ring. That means there's still a chance for me. I'll call you tonight."

"Don't—"

But he'd turned on his heel, swaggered down the aisle, and exited through the rear doors. She shook her head. *What a mess.*

Connor's heart pounded as he strode through the outer door of the church and across the parking lot. Who did this guy think he was, whispering in Brianna's ear? Didn't he get it? She'd left him behind. She was in love, and it wasn't with *Kurt*.

As Connor jerked the driver's door open on the Impala, his neck grew hotter. If Kurt thought he'd take her away, he'd better rethink. But how to stop him. The guy was built like Hercules. So, why wouldn't she fall for him?

In the rearview mirror, he spotted Brianna exit the church building, her steps graceful as a young willow tree waving in the breeze. She was the woman he loved, and yet he'd not moved past the pain of being left at the altar. How pathetic to still be so unsure of himself after so many months. They weren't kids anymore. *And I can't lose her again.*

Connor jumped out of the car and opened the passenger door for her. "Your chariot awaits, fair maiden."

She giggled. "Why did you leave?"

He closed the door. With heavy steps, he trod to the driver's side and dropped behind the wheel. He started the engine, then glanced at her. Wispy strands of blonde hair brushed over her high cheekbones. Her pale rosy lips called to him, but her eyes captured his and demanded an answer. "I thought you and Kurt might want privacy."

"Connor. I told you. There was nothing in the relationship. He was there when I needed a friend. You, of all people, should understand that." Her brows rose.

As he pulled out of the parking lot, Connor reached over and took her hand. Things would work out this time. *I'll make sure they do.*

On Christmas Eve, Connor hurried to leave his apartment. Time to rid their lives of Kurt. He'd been hovering around Brianna like a honeybee at a hive. The man would never give up without a fight. He'd all but invited himself to the O'Sullivans' holiday dinner. Gracious to a fault, Brianna's parents had acquiesced.

Connor parked in the driveway next to Kurt's oversized, black Ford F350, looking like it had overdosed on steroids. *Super!* Well, his plan to take Brianna away would end tonight.

As he got out of the car, Brianna dashed around the corner of the house and up to him. "I'm *so* glad you're here."

"Why are you outside?"

"Making myself scarce." She grinned.

He raised her chin with his index finger and gazed into her pale blue eyes. His lips lowered to hers. Warmth flowed through his body.

When he ended the kiss, her jaw slackened, and her eyes rounded. "You've *never* kissed me like *that*."

He chuckled. "I've wanted to since you came home. Before we go in, take a walk with me." He opened his long tawny-brown coat with the lambskin liner and wrapped one side around her shoulders. "This should keep you warm."

As she slipped her arm around his waist and snuggled next to his ribs, the fragrance of roses filled the air. He held her close. She still wore the rose perfume he'd given her their last Christmas together. The scent suited her.

They strolled to the bank of the bayou. The gate swung closed behind them with a kerchunk.

Brianna waved at several black-bellied whistling ducks as they flew over in V formation. "I love the way they sing as they fly."

He turned and pulled her into his arms, closing the coat tightly around them. "Speaking of love...I have a very important question for you, Miss O'Sullivan."

She tilted her head and squinted at him. "What is it?"

He kissed her nose and then backed away from her. "Will you marry this idiot who should have moved heaven and earth to find you when you ran away?" He pulled a ring from his pocket and held it in front of her. The heart-shaped diamond her mother had returned to him four years ago sparkled as the sun's rays hit it. Connor lifted her left hand and slipped the ring on her finger before she had time to answer. "Please?"

Brianna's mouth opened in slow motion. She gawked from her finger to his eyes. Her arms flew up and grasped him around his neck. She squeezed, and he wrapped the coat around them again. "Yes, yes, yes, yes. I didn't think you'd ever take me back." She rose on her tiptoes and kissed him.

He covered her lips with his, and their kiss deepened. As he enveloped his coat tighter around them, his consciousness blocked out everything but Brianna in his arms.

The gate to the backyard banged open. They spun to face it. The O'Sullivans rushed toward them, Kurt right behind.

Brianna's mother smiled at Kurt as she threw a jacket around Brianna and hugged her daughter. "Your idea worked, Kurt. I'm so glad you called to tell us you were moving to Houston. A little competition was all Connor needed."

Kurt winked at Brianna's mother. "Told you it was no problem." He gazed at Brianna. "I knew I wasn't the man for her almost from the start, and I couldn't stand the heartache in her eyes."

With his mouth agape, Connor faced Kurt. "So, you all planned this?" He stared at Mr. and Mrs. O'Sullivan, hands over their mouths, holding back laughter. Then Connor jerked his head toward Brianna. She mirrored his stunned expression. He burst into laughter and turned to Kurt. "Man, you had my green-eyed monster this close to decking you." He held up his hand, the thumb and index finger an inch apart.

Kurt thrust out his hand, and the two men shook. "Just be good to Brianna. And don't let her get away this time." He grinned at her.

"Don't worry. I won't." Connor pulled his new/old fiancée to him and reclaimed her lips, accompanied by a chorus of cheers.

The End

Whoso findeth a wife findeth a good thing, and obtaineth favour of the LORD.

Proverbs 18:22

Painting
Rainbows

Painting Rainbows

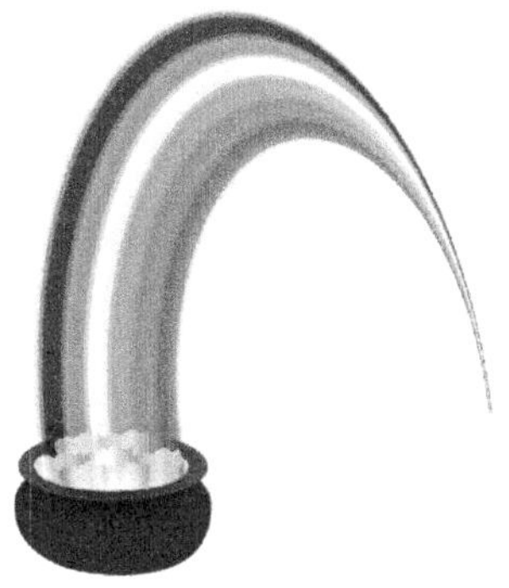

Genre: Fantasy

Each time a rainbow reveals where the leprechaun Finian O'Conner has hidden his pots of gold, he must run to check on them. He's tired of tourists to his homeland in Galway, Ireland, trying to catch him and make him give up his treasure. To escape the nuisance, he transports himself and his gold to Middle Earth where he encounters an artistic elf on the edge of a forest.

Painting Rainbows

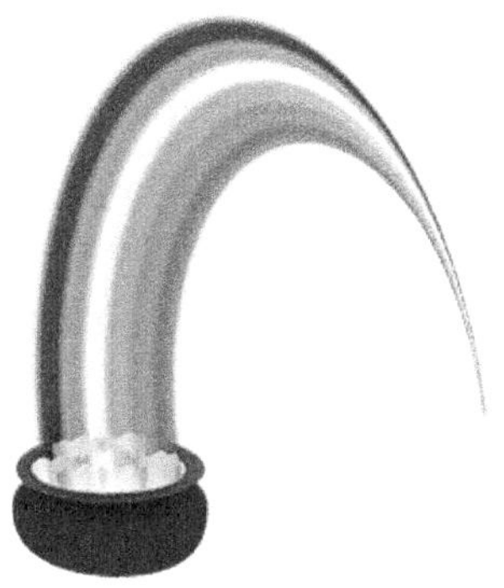

Finian O'Conner stretched his arms and neck to his full three feet to loosen his muscles after his bumpy transport with his pots of gold to Middle Earth from Galway, Ireland. 'Twas a sad thing when a leprechaun had to leave his ancestral country where he'd abode for the past two hundred years. But he'd finally had enough and escaped the treasure-hunting tourists who plagued his homeland. Every time a rainbow appeared, they were off to discover where he'd hidden his cache. And appear the rainbows did...often. *Too* often.

The last thief had almost gotten away with one pot. It had happened more times than he cared to remember. Could age be creeping up on him? He scratched his head. Surely not. He was but a mere two centuries old. Always being on the lookout for those pesky rainbows and having to rush to hide the vessels in a new hole over and over wore him to a frazzle. Why did those bows have to point to his hiding place, anyway? He glanced up at the sky. Not a cloud in sight. He grinned. A haven at last.

Finian brushed off his Kelly-green suit, straightened his orange bowtie. He adjusted his dark green top hat upon his rusty orange mop of curly hair and then took an inventory of his ten heaping pots. "Ah. None missing. One fat tub for every twenty years of collecting. Now, where would be a secure location for my treasure?" He gazed over the sea of glittering coins and beyond the meadow he'd landed in, to the edge of the forest. "Under those brambles beneath the trees." Ideal, since he wasn't familiar with his surroundings yet. 'Twould be an easy spot to remember.

With a flick of his wrist, the gleaming pots flew to the woods. Seconds later, Finian stood with a toothy smile on his lips as he brushed his hands off, though he'd not touched a speck of dirt. Such a fine gift, his magic. No manual labor for this leprechaun. And no one would ever guess what lay under those bushes.

"Now where might a famished leprechaun find a bit of corned beef and cabbage to eat and a pint of ale?" He'd have to find a suitable cottage to stay in as well. Then he'd decide if he wanted the humans who lived there to know he'd chosen to share the place with them...or not. Either way, he'd have fun with some innocent pranks. What kind of people lived in this new land?

As he stepped out of the bushes and into the meadow, his jaw lowered at the sight of wildflowers in every hue as far as he could see. He'd not noticed them in the rush to hide his treasure. "Sure, and my lady fair back home would love this place." He already missed the strawberry blonde lass of a leprechaun he'd left behind. But keeping his treasure safe had to come first.

Yards away sat an elf clothed in pale blue robes poised on a tall stool, paintbrush in hand. The long-limbed creature faced a canvas. From where had this lanky lad come? " 'Twasn't there a wee bit ago."

Finian approached the elf from behind and viewed the painting. A lovely meadow landscape with a woods next to it. The scene could be the field and forest behind them. And the canvas stopped right at the spot he'd left his gold.

The elf stood and turned. From a height twice that of the tallest leprechaun ever known, he peered down. His shiny, pale blue eyes scanned from Finian's green top hat to his black, silver-buckled shoes. 'Twas as though the creature could see right through to the heart. The leprechaun shuddered.

Pointed ears poked out from the elf's long, straight white locks, which draped around his shoulders. An intricate band of woven bright silver adorned his forehead and disappeared under his hair at the temples.

The tall creature's brows rose. "Hello. Are you new in our land, Mr...?"

"I am." Finian checked the area for more elves. None. He tucked his thumbs in his orange suspenders. "Finian O'Conner, here. Arrived a moment ago, and I'll be lookin' for lodgin' if ye be askin'. And who might ye be?"

The fair creature smiled. "Vorilandar Greystone. At your service, sir." He gave a quick nod.

Finian's eyes narrowed. Was that a snicker behind the elf's grin, now? What was so humorous?

Vorilandar laid his brush and palate on the easel's shelf. He touched Finian's shoulder. "Come with me. I'll direct you to a comfortable inn where you can get settled and find food."

The following day, Finian ventured back to the meadow in front of the forest. A soft mist, like thin, low-flying clouds, drifted up from the ground and across his path. In the distance, Vorilandar sat with his easel and paints. Odd to be out here painting in this weather.

Before Finian could reach the elf, the sun came out, and a rainbow followed. The colored arch spanned the sky and plunged to where Finian had buried his pots of gold. He darted to the woods and circled around to his hiding place. Whew! Untouched. But since the bow pointed to the spot, he'd still have to move them.

An hour later, Finian emerged from the woodland to find Vorilandar still in place. "Must be working on his picture of the meadow." As Finian neared, the elf made a wide blue brushstroke through the sky on the canvas, covering the top half of the painting. Must not have been happy with the clouds he made. "Ahem."

Vorilandar turned to Finian. "Good morning. Did you find the lodge to your liking?"

"It was pleasant. Yes, it will do until I find a proper dwelling. Thank you. Nice painting."

The elf resumed his work.

Not much on conversation, but perhaps they could be friends. Finian cinched his lips to one side. He needed someone to talk to so far from home.

Each day of the following week, he strolled through the meadow and parked himself under a golden mallorn tree in front of the woods. He observed as the elf worked, adding clouds and a rainbow to the canvas. Always the same view. Vorilandar had no imagination. Always the same field with the same forest beyond, and always one of those pesky bows.

A bright rainbow formed in the heavens over Finian's head. *And here I go again.* Every time the elf added a bow to his painting, clouds floated in, and a colored arch appeared overhead. Might be the climate here. He'd have to move those pots again.

Finian jumped up and ran to his treasure. No wonder Vorilandar created so many rainbows on his landscapes. Pictures of meadows and bows must be popular with the residents here.

The next day, right before he'd reached the elf, a rainbow traversed the sky and settled where Finian had reburied his vessels of gold the day before. Now he'd have to dart off and relocate them. *Again.* "This is ridiculous." This was why he'd left his home in Ireland. The only difference was, he'd never seen any humans here lollygaggin' around to catch him. "What's going on?"

A month went by with the same routine each day. "I have to find out if rain with rainbows is the daily, year-round weather pattern here in Middle Earth." He'd also find out why Vorilandar fashioned the same scene all the time.

As Finian entered the flower-laden field, Vorilandar painted in his usual position. Sure enough, a bow materialized over the artist but faded before proceeding to the ground. "I don't care if it lands right atop my treasure. I *will* get to the bottom of this." But he had to think first. How to approach the subject? He meandered through the wildflowers and dropped himself onto the grass with his back against the silver trunk of the mallorn.

The elf didn't seem to notice him. Finian studied the picture. The meadow, the forest, a large tree with deep yellow leaves. Blue sky, but a faint streak across it. His brows rumpled. He gaped up at the foliage under which he sat. Its silver branches, loaded with sparkling gold leaves the size of platters spread out above him.

He jumped to his feet and strode to Vorilandar.

The elf turned to face Finian. "May I help you, Mr. O'Conner?"

"Yes. Why do you always paint the same thing? The same scene. Colorful field with a woodland to the side. And the mallorn tree."

Without a word, Vorilandar spun and brushed in the rest of the rainbow, bringing it down to the woods.

Finian watched as the colored arch above his head continued its path to the same spot in the thicket as in the picture.

"My dear, Mr. O'Conner. Aren't you afraid someone will find your pots of gold while you stand here and question me?"

Finian shook his head. "I haven't seen a single human enter those thickets since I've been here. Nor another elf in the area. Only you, these paintings, and those vexatious rainbows." He shoved his fist upward with his index finger pointed to the sky. "Every time you add one of those irksome bows to your picture, another appears up there. And it reveals exactly where I've buried my treasure. What I don't understand is, how do you know? And...you've been facing away from the timberland. How can you paint what's behind you?"

"As the high elf prince of the deep woodlands, I have the gift of foresight. I need not see the trees to reproduce them here." He waved his arm toward the canvas. "Nor do I need to see where you've hidden your stash to direct a rainbow to it. I know where they'll be before you do."

Finian's eyes snapped to the painting as Prince Vorilandar picked up his brush and stroked in a double arch in the sky. The second rainbow stretched over them and ended in the same location as the first, on the tree under which Finian had concealed his pots.

"Why do you betray me? What have I done to you?"

"There is no betrayal. I've not led any humans to your stockpile. Finian O'Conner, you are too greedy, even for a leprechaun. You should have used your abundant wealth to help others, not hoard it."

Finian's heart pinched from the spoken truth. Heat rose in his neck and traveled to his face. As his chin sagged, his outstretched, pointed ears burned. Vorilandar was right. Close to two hundred years of hoarding, and not once had he given any coins to the poor people with whom he'd lived through the years in his homeland.

He peeked up at the elf. "Why did you not let anyone find the gold? Why did you not take it for yourself or allow elfkind to have it?"

The prince pointed up to the mallorn leaves behind Finian. "We have all the gold we need right here."

The clouds dispersed, and Finian lifted his eyes to the tree. Its leaves glittered in the sun as no golden coin ever could. He smiled. His heart, which had been cold and hard, warmed. He turned to the prince. "I'm glad I came to the woodland realm. You've taught me an important lesson."

A glow came to Vorilandar's face. "I had hoped I could, Finian. Now we can be friends."

"My lady fair, back in Galway, tried to tell me I'd become a miser, but I refused to listen. I'm lonesome for her and my people. Time to go back to Ireland. I'll leave half of the pots behind in your care, my princely friend. Use it as you think best."

Prince Vorilandar held out his hand. "There is no necessity for gold here, my dear Finian. Use it where needed in your homeland. And you'll always be welcomed in my woodland home."

"Maybe someday soon, I'll bring a certain ginger-haired lassie with me? This would be a perfect place for a honeymoon. Complete with rainbows."

The End

So is he that layeth up treasure for himself, and is not rich toward God. Luke 12:21

For where your treasure is, there will your heart be also. Matthew 6:21

The Masque

The Masque

Genre: Suspense

Nathan Ainsley's brother, Noah, has decided to hold a big party to celebrate his promotion in the law firm he has worked at since graduation from law school. Nathan has no problem with the celebration to honor his brother, but why did it have to be a masquerade party.

After picking out his costume and leaving the shop, Nathan sees the woman he loves knocked down and shot in front of the bank. As the getaway car speeds off, he catches a glimpse of his brother at the wheel. It can't be.

The Masque

Nathan Ainsley whispered in the costume shop's changing room, "Why did it have to be a masquerade?" He could understand the celebration of his older brother Noah's promotion seven days away, but why a silly dress-up party?

Nathan took a last gander at himself in the Zorro outfit he'd settled on and pursed his lips. He'd waited too long to find something, and now— "I look ridiculous."

As he paid the fee and left the shop, he grumbled. "I don't care what anyone thinks." He slung the garment bag over his shoulder.

Who was he kidding? He *did* care. He'd deck the first person who snickered at him. Especially if it was Noah. Nathan chuckled.

He'd been an average student throughout high school and college. And the girls never considered him a dark-haired hunk as they did his brother, even though they could pass for twins. Must have been the confidence Noah exuded. He'd been the super-smart one in the family, an honor student, and all-conference quarterback at the University of Chicago. He'd flaunted every achievement he'd ever accomplished. Now, he was to become a partner in a prestigious law firm.

But why did his brother have to pick a masquerade? Nathan strode across the street toward the parking lot. Why not a dinner in one of those fancy restaurants he frequented? No-o-o...that wasn't Noah's style. The flamboyant brother had to do things in a big way, different from everyone else. He lived for the attention.

Get over it, man. Olivia might like the outfit.

Nathan entered the lot but stopped. "*Drat.*" He'd left his car keys on the counter. He did an about-face and headed back to the street.

Olivia never criticized his choices. She'd encourage him. Hers was the opinion that mattered. Not once had she cast any doubt on her faith in what he could accomplish. Or on her affection for him. His best friend and confidant, she was the woman he wanted to spend the rest of his life with.

As he neared the shop, he pictured Olivia. Five feet, ten inches tall, the same height as his. Striking long, auburn hair and green eyes. His heart pounded. Yes. He was ready to propose to her.

Olivia strolled into view on the other side of the bank building they'd reach within a minute. She waved, quickened her steps, and arrived at the entrance several feet before him.

Two men in fancy party masks rushed out with sacks in their hands. One man slammed into Olivia, and she fell to the sidewalk. When she peered up at him, the other man pointed a gun and fired.

Both men jumped into a waiting car, which peeled rubber as it escaped the scene.

"Olivia!" Nathan threw the costume to the ground, dashed to her collapsed body, and plunged to his knees. Her pulse was weak. He flipped his cell out of his pocket and pressed 9-1-1.

As the red blotch on her shoulder spread, Nathan answered the emergency responder's questions. He hung up. *God, please let her live.*

Time traveled in slow motion, and a crowd gathered while he waited for the paramedics. Prickles slid down the back of his neck.

A stranger punched in numbers on his phone. "I'll call again. They should've been here by now."

Nathan nodded.

"Here." A woman from behind the gawkers pushed through. "Try to stop the bleeding with this." She handed him a package of tissues.

Nathan tore the pack open and pressed the block of absorbent paper on top of Olivia's wound.

"I picked up your garment bag." The lady who'd given him the tissues laid it on the ground next to him.

"Thank you." He couldn't care less about the stupid costume. Nathan kept light pressure on the tissues as he listened for the siren. "What's keeping those paramedics?" He peeked at his watch. How long had it been?

Olivia moaned.

"Hang on, honey. Help's on the way." He hoped. The driver of the car had resembled his brother. But it couldn't be.

Sirens blared in the distance. "Finally."

The ambulance careened around the corner, lights flashing, and stopped with a screech. Two paramedics hopped out and assessed the damage to Olivia's shoulder. "Folks, give her space to breathe."

Once the paramedics transferred her to a gurney, they hoisted her into the vehicle. Sirens pierced the air once more as the ambulance sped for the hospital.

Nathan raced back to the costume shop, retrieved his keys, and ran to his car. Twenty minutes later, he arrived at the hospital.

Half an hour went by in the waiting room before he was told he could see Olivia. He darted into her cubicle. Olivia reclined on a gurney, her head on the pillow, and her arm in a sling. "You're awake. Man, I didn't think they'd ever let me back here. I was so worried."

"I'm okay. The doctor said the bullet grazed my shoulder. The shock caused me to pass out."

A nurse with glassy-eyes, as though at the end of her twelve-hour shift, came in and handed Olivia a medicine cup and water. "This will ease the pain."

Olivia pushed herself into a sitting position. "Ow!" She swung her legs over the edge of the gurney.

His emotions churned inside as she groaned. She was so fragile.

She swallowed the pills and smiled at him, but the lines in her forehead told him something more than pain bothered her.

The nurse took the cup from her. "Don't stand. You may be dizzy." After Olivia nodded, the clinician left.

"Nathan, did you see your brother? He drove the car."

"What? No. It couldn't be." Could it? Like most people, Noah had done a lot of things he shouldn't have through the years. But to be involved with someone who shot Olivia? Impossible.

"Yes. It was Noah. He was the driver. Didn't you see him as the car sped away?"

He blinked at her. "I—"

Nathan's brother slipped through the part in the curtain into the exam room. "Hey, Olivia. We were at the restaurant next door to the bank."

As his best friends, Cal and Kevin, stood in the gap of the privacy curtains, Noah held up a hand to stop them from entering. He faced Olivia. "Heard what happened to you from another customer." He stretched his arm across Nathan's back but kept his eyes on her. "I take it you're not as bad off as they thought."

"I guess not." She glowered at Noah's two friends. "The guy was a rotten shot."

Nathan disentangled himself from his brother's arm. Should he make an accusation or not? If Olivia saw him too—which of them fired the gun?

Daggers flew from her eyes to Cal's. "*You* were the one who ran into me outside the bank. You lost your mask in the process."

Nathan glared at Cal. She'd seen his face. That means Noah *had been* the driver. Nathan's head spun. He'd been so concerned about Olivia, he hadn't paid attention to the men who assaulted her. It also meant—he turned to Kevin—*he* shot her.

Noah latched onto Nathan's shoulder. "Olivia's mistaken. She's distraught, not thinking clearly."

An ER security guard stepped into the room. "Is there a problem here?" He scanned their faces.

Nathan wiggled out of his brother's grip and took Olivia's hand.

The guard eyed the other three. "This patient has too many visitors. I suggest you three return to the waiting area."

The day after the masquerade, Nathan paced his apartment. He and Olivia had arrived late and left early. Too many questions if they had skipped the party. They hadn't spoken to his brother once.

Why hadn't he told the police Noah drove the getaway car? Nathan bit his lower lip. It would have crushed his parents.

Nathan stepped into his closet and covered the Zorro costume with the plastic bag it had come in. It'd been awkward to avoid Noah for the entire evening, but they'd managed. Either Cal or Kevin never took off their masks, or they weren't there. Strange.

Olivia sure was beautiful in her emerald senorita gown.

"Where's the mask?" He searched his apartment but couldn't find it. "Hope the costume shop doesn't charge me an arm and a leg to replace it."

A vision of Olivia, at the masquerade, in her gown with black trim materialized before him. She was beautiful, even with a sling to match the dress. He laughed. When he'd proposed on the balcony of the banquet hall, the expression on her face was priceless. What a kiss she'd given him.

His mind drifted back to the ER. She'd been so sure who had knocked her down. They should've told the officer who came to take their statements who they'd recognized. Olivia gave her side of the story and left that out. What could he do but keep quiet too? She'd told him later she didn't mention his brother's involvement. *For my sake.*

As he neared the front door, Nathan halted. He *may* have seen Noah's friends at the party. There were a couple of men who had the same masks he'd seen at the robbery.

Nathan picked up his keys from the foyer table to leave for work at the accounting firm. He stared into the mirror on the wall. "We can't let them get away with it." He'd have to talk to her. They had to inform the police after her checkup today.

At five, he left the office and picked up Olivia from home for her doctor's appointment. As they exited the physician's office, she moved her shoulder in a circle. "See? Almost back to normal. *Ouch*. Well. Like I said, almost."

They walked to the elevator. "Let's celebrate *almost* healed." He pressed the down button.

"What kind of celebration do you have in mind, my dear fiancé?"

"Dinner this Friday at your favorite restaurant?"

She took a deep breath. "Gibson's? Sounds wonderful."

When the elevator door opened, they stepped inside. He touched the circle marked Lobby, the doors slid shut, and he spun to take her hand. "Olivia, I was so afraid I'd lost you the day the bank was robbed. I'm relieved you're okay."

As the car descended, his fingers brushed the side of her face to her jawline. He outlined her lips with his thumb, then leaned in and kissed her. As she inched her hand around his waist, he pulled her to his chest.

The car stopped, the doors opened, and an older couple raised their brows. Nathan released Olivia, and they stepped out. Her cheeks turned a rosy pink. He grinned. "We've a lifetime of kisses ahead of us. I should've proposed to you lo-o-ong before now."

A giggle escaped Olivia's lips. "I sure wish you had."

They hurried through the parking lot to the car and got in. He twisted to face her. "Let's talk about what happened the day you were shot."

Her emerald eyes widened and filled with tears. "As I said in the ER, I saw Noah in the car as they drove away, and I recognized Cal when he bumped into me and knocked his mask off his face."

"I caught a glimpse of Noah too. We have to go to the police with the information."

"But he's your brother, Nathan. What will it do to you and your family?"

"Everything will be all right. The truth needs to be told."

As Noah and Cal sat at the kitchen table in Kevin's apartment, Noah was ready to jump out of his skin. He buried his face in his hands, elbows on the table. Had Olivia seen him in the getaway car? In the two weeks since the robbery, the police hadn't shown up on his doorstep. What would he do if they did? He'd lose his job for sure. She'd seen Cal's face, and the way she glared at Kevin, she suspected he'd shot her.

"I haven't been questioned by the authorities yet." Cal let out a deep sigh. "Anyone else?"

Noah rubbed the stubble on his cleft chin. "No." Nate hadn't said one word to him about the robbery, though their eyes had met as the car pulled away. *Why hadn't either of them said anything?* He'd tiptoed on eggshells since the theft.

"Not yet." Kevin scowled at Noah. "I suggest we kidnap your brother and his fiancée, just in case. We know she, at least, recognized Cal. We'll hold them somewhere isolated until the boss decides what to do with them. Remember, with the juicy info he has on us, he holds the cards."

"You're crazy if you think I'll put Nate in danger. *No.* We'll keep quiet and do nothing. Not a finger is to be lifted against my brother. Or Olivia."

Kevin jumped from the chair. "When we left the ER, you said we'd deal with them."

"I was upset. What I said then and what we'll do now are two different things." Flames flew from Noah's eyes to the much smaller man. Kevin was spineless. *He wouldn't dare go against me.*

Cal drummed his fingers on the worn Formica, then stopped. "This is a royal mess." He sat back and crossed his arms over his chest.

"*Guys,*" Noah's eyes flashed from Cal to Kevin, "the blackmailer doesn't know my brother or Olivia was there, right? As long as they don't say anything, let's not make matters worse. Maybe this blackmailer is finished with us after such a rich haul. Has he contacted you again?"

Kevin popped a beer and guzzled it. "Not yet."

Noah rose and headed to the door. "I have to go. Come on, Cal. I'll drop you off."

His friend followed Noah out of Kevin's apartment without a word. They reached Noah's BMW and slipped into the front seats.

As he drove, sweat formed on Noah's brow. A block from Cal's home, Noah pulled into a side street and parked. He turned off the engine.

"Hey." Cal whipped his head around to face Noah. "What's up? Fay's holding dinner for me. I told her I'd be home an hour ago."

Noah grimaced. "Kevin's suggestion to kidnap Nate and Olivia...you don't agree, do you?"

"Of course not. We're in enough trouble as it is."

Noah gave Cal a weak smile. "Good. You were so quiet in there, I wasn't sure where your mind was. I have an idea to end this blackmail problem."

"So, what's the solution?" Cal's forehead showed deep worry lines.

"I haven't thought it through yet. Give me a day or two. Let's get you home to your wife and kids. Keep things cool."

On Friday, Nathan and Olivia ate dinner on the balcony of Gibson's Italian Restaurant overlooking the Chicago River. After they'd finished their steaks in the crisp evening air, he retrained his eyes from the busy city to Olivia. "Last night, I was approached by Detective Dane Gregory. He's a client of ours at the accounting firm and an old friend."

Olivia's brows pinched.

"You met him at my parents' thirtieth wedding anniversary party two months ago, remember?"

"Oh, yes. The silvery gray-haired gentleman who seemed suspicious of every guest." She tittered.

"He does come across that way to people who don't know him. Occupational hazard." Nathan cleared his throat. "He told me he thought Noah had been involved in a few burglaries."

Olivia's eyes widened. "I haven't—"

The waiter delivered goblets of chocolate mousse to each of them. Nathan touched her hand as it rested next to her dessert. "We'll talk later."

They finished their meal and left.

When they arrived at Olivia's apartment, they strolled to the bench in a garden at the front of the building and sat. He circled her shoulders with his arm and pulled her to him. "Last night, Dane explained what the authorities have suspected with two robberies at the bank where you were shot."

She leaned her head back and gazed at him. "I haven't told anyone. Did you tell him who we saw the day of the robbery?"

"Yes. I hated to. But it was the right thing to do."

"Oh, Nathan." She nestled her head under his chin.

"Now, for the hard part." He took her hands in his and faced her.

"What do you mean, the *hard* part?"

"Dane needs my help. They haven't made any arrests because they want evidence on the ringleader who must work at the bank. Arrangements were made for me to take over a temporary position there and be '*his eyes*,' as Dane phrased it."

"Nathan, you're not—"

"I've agreed to do it, Olivia. I'll be fine. Dane's promised to help my brother. He's convinced there's more to the story than the obvious."

Early Monday morning, Nathan's intent gaze bored holes into the eyes of the reflection in the mirror behind the bathroom sink. "What were you thinking? You're no private eye. You're an accountant." He wiped the residue of shaving lather off his face and entered the walk-in closet.

He lifted the hanger with the steel-gray suit he'd chosen to wear for the first day at the bank and carried it into the bedroom. As he laid it over the valet stand, something dark on the floor behind the bed caught his attention. One of his socks must've gone astray.

Nathan stooped to retrieve the item and let out a guffaw. "So, *that's* where you went." He grabbed the soft black mask he'd worn to the masquerade party. "Well, I had to pay an exorbitant price to replace you, so I guess you're mine now. Just what I needed...a prop from *The Mask of Zorro*." He grimaced.

"It was a terrific movie we watched last month, but I sure didn't feel like a *caped crusader* at the masque." He stared at the mask. *Hmm.*

Since he wore it, he'd had more confidence. He held the black cloth in front of him. "Shall I save you for encouragement?" The limp piece of fabric dangled in the air with no reply.

He laid the mask on a shelf inside his chifferobe and picked up his insignia of rank from the time he served as a sergeant in the Army. He returned it to the tray and took out his Commendation Medal. *V for Valor*. For six years he'd trained. "Thank God for the skills." Dane had often told him he should've joined the force after he left the service. He laid the medal back down.

Nathan's fingers grazed over his badge for expert rifle marksmanship. Police work wasn't what God had intended him to do. He was sure of it. "Still, I can do this job for them." He closed the door to the closet-like piece of walnut furniture.

He dressed and checked his appearance twice in a full-length mirror on the bedroom door. "Yeah. Today, you're a banker. No one will be the wiser."

Before dawn a few days later, Noah waited outside Detective Gregory's home. He searched the street to make sure no one had followed him. What else could he do? He needed help, and he'd known Dane Gregory before Nate ever joined the Army. No more bank robberies. Who knew where it might lead next?

Noah sucked in a breath and sneaked around the house to the back yard. The neighbor's dog barked as he knocked on the door.

The kitchen light flicked on, and Mrs. Gregory peered out the nine-pane window.

She turned on the porch light. "Honey, a young man is out here on the deck."

Dane strode into the room and snatched the door open. "Noah, we were just talking about you."

"Huh? Who is we?" Noah's brows furrowed.

"Your brother and me."

"Nate's here? Why?" *He ratted on me.* No. His brother wouldn't, not after keeping quiet all this time. But then, he had strong ethics.

"Come on in." Dane pulled Noah into the kitchen and led him to the living room.

After Detective Gregory explained what the department investigators had uncovered with Nate's help at the bank during the past three weeks, Noah confessed his part in the thefts. "I'm also being blackmailed."

"So, Dane's hunch was right." Nate blew out a stream of air between his lips. "For the life of me, I couldn't understand why you'd gotten involved in a robbery. What about Cal and Kevin? Does this guy have something on them too?"

Noah hung his head. "Not sure what he has on Kevin, but Cal was with me at the lounge after the hockey game to celebrate the Blackhawk's victory. The two young women came to our table. We were pretty loaded and took them for older than they were. They fooled the guy who checked IDs at the door too." Noah closed his eyes and let out a heavy sigh.

Mrs. Gregory brought in a tray of steaming coffee mugs and breakfast pastries. She offered a plate to Noah.

"No, thank you." Noah's hands jittered as he took a cup and sipped.

"We bought the girls drinks and got up to leave. The doors burst open and—" He took another drink. "The next thing we knew, we were in squad cars and hauled off to the precinct."

The detective nodded. "I remember that bust."

Noah pulled his lips to one side. "If it hadn't been for you, Cal and I would've had our lives ruined."

"The facts were obvious." Dane took a bite of cream cheese Danish and returned it to his plate. "You two didn't know the girls were underage. We had the dive under surveillance and saw what was going on. A warning sufficed in your case."

The detective finished his pastry. "We'd better wrap this up fast. Nathan and I have business to attend to at the bank."

Noah took a last sip and placed the mug on the coffee table. "Cal and I got together with Kevin later that night and told him what had happened. We'd been close friends for a long time. We trusted him. The next day I received an email saying I was to contact Kevin and follow the instructions he'd been given, or my boss would be informed of the lounge incident. I panicked. You know what a prestigious firm I work for." Noah glanced at Nate. "I'd lose everything. Cal and I assumed whoever had sent the message had something on Kevin as well.

"It wasn't until after this last job when he shot Olivia I started to wonder if he was in league with the blackmailer. Kevin let some clues slip. Sounded like a bank employee is behind this."

Dane and Nate eyed each other.

Noah continued. "Cal had been scared to death he'd lose his wife and kids if she found out he had flirted with and bought alcohol for two girls at a lounge. It would've been my fault since I'm the one who talked him into going with me." Noah clamped his lips shut for a moment. "I can't let the guy use us to commit crimes anymore. No matter what."

"Listen, Noah." Dane slapped him on the shoulder. "The first thing you'll do is contact your boss. I'll go in with you and explain what happened at the lounge. You can voice your fears over your job and position. Also, tell him you wanted to protect Cal."

Noah's jaw slackened. His forehead moistened. He gritted his teeth.

Dane cocked his head. "Neither you nor Cal have a record. So unless someone made a video of you in the lounge or at the police station, there is no proof. With your law firm's reputation, your boss will be happy no arrest was reported nor any news of a blackmailed employee. He also wouldn't want any mention of one of their lawyers being a driver in a bank robbery."

If only his boss didn't have to know. Too late for that. Noah pressed his lips together again.

Nate wiped the pastry crumbs off his mouth. "Noah. No one else has to know any of this. We planned to talk to you before you showed up. I asked Dane if there was any way to help you out of this mess. He said yes."

"Kevin, on the other hand," Dane pursed his lips, "is suspected of other crimes."

Noah's mouth lowered again. "Kevin? Wimpy, slow-witted Kevin?"

The detective narrowed his eyes. "He's been used. No proof yet, but the signs are there."

"You need to do this, Noah." Nate patted his back. "Tell your boss. The repercussions won't be as bad as you've imagined."

"They won't." Dane finished his coffee and rose. "I know your boss. He's a fair man."

"Big brother, you'll have plenty of time to prove your worth to the firm. They'll see they didn't make a mistake with your promotion."

If only he were as confident as his little brother. Noah stood. He'd do it anyway. He shook Nate's hand.

"Oh. I almost forgot." He faced the detective. "Kevin wanted to kidnap Olivia and Nate, let the blackmailer decide what to do with them. Enough was enough."

"We'll take a complete statement from you." Dane led Nate and Noah to the back door. "Noah, go to the precinct. Tell them I told you to wait for me. I'll be there within the hour. It's time for us to have a talk with Cal now. We'll haul Kevin in for interrogation. I'm sure he'll give us the information we need to arrest the ringleader."

Nathan and Olivia joined Noah for dinner the night after the trial and conviction of the blackmailer and Kevin. What a relief to know Noah hadn't turned to a life of crime. "You had me worried for a while with the robbery and your obsession with the masquerade party. Particularly when I saw a couple of the same masks at the party like the ones Cal and Kevin wore."

"Yeah. The masks at the bank heist were Kevin's idea." Noah laughed. "I can see where the connection between the masks and the bank robbery comes in. But it's a stretch." He chuckled. "Thanks for the faith you've had in me, no matter how bad it looked. The expense for your wedding in the spring is on me."

Olivia opened her mouth to speak, but he held up his hand to stop her. "It's the least I can do to show how grateful I am to have a brother who has my back and a beautiful soon-to-be sister-in-law who loves Nate enough not to want him or his family hurt. I've no wife or kids of my own...yet." He grinned. "Need to find a great girl like you first." He lifted his stemmed water glass to her. "So, I can afford to spend the money to get you two hitched. With your parents both gone and you an only child—"

Tears filled her eyes. She laid her hand on Noah's.

Nathan wrapped his arm around her shoulders. "Thank you, Noah. So tell me. How did Cal come out after he confessed to Fay?"

"I went with him and said it was my idea. She was upset, as expected. But when I told her we only bought them drinks, didn't know they were underage, and then we'd been blackmailed, it was as I expected. The remorse on Cal's face got to her. She forgave him. They'll have a rough year until Cal proves himself again, I suspect. It'll work out in the end because they love each other."

Nathan could almost see the wheels turning in his brother's head.

"Hmm...Fay has an older, single sister. They've tried to set up a blind date for us a few times." His brows arched. "I'd better check her out."

The couple smiled.

"Hey, you two. Now that you're in such a relaxed mood, I've a suggestion for your wedding and reception."

Olivia's shoulders stiffened under Nathan's arm. She pressed her eyes closed, brows rumpled, and took in a quick gulp of air.

He rubbed her back. *Oh, no. Here it comes. Noah's going to suggest a—*

"Why not make your theme a masquerade? You and Nate can dress as Zorro and his lady?"

Nathan held back a laugh. "It's worth a thought, sweetheart. I already own a mask. You'd be gorgeous in a Spanish wedding gown." He gave her a sheepish look. "That mask is a bad influence."

The End

He that covereth his sins shall not prosper: but whoso confesseth and forsaketh them shall have mercy. Proverbs 28:13

Don't Step
in the
Fairy Ring

Don't Step in the Fairy Ring

Genre: Fantasy

High school senior Tara Flynn is head-over-heels for her twin brother's best friend, Shane O'Leary. But Mac Seaberg is the one who keeps vying for her attention. Tara wants nothing to do with Mac, especially when he ridicules her for believing in fairies. Is stepping in a fairy ring made of mushrooms really bad luck?

Don't Step in the Fairy Ring

Tara Flynn riveted Mac's gray eyes with a cold, crystal blue-eyed stare as she grabbed his arm and pulled him away from the delicate circle of mushrooms. "That's a fairy ring, Mac. You should never disturb them. You don't want bad luck, do you?"

She stepped to the side of the three-feet-wide circle of fungus in the field behind her parents' farm, next to the woods.

Eighteen-year-old Mac Seaberg held his booted foot over the ring of delicate mushrooms again and snickered at her. The wind whipped his shaggy sandy-blond hair around his head.

"*Stop*, Mac." Tara slapped his arm and pulled him to the ground.

"You don't want to tempt fate again." A year earlier, he'd cackled while he stomped the delicate white mushrooms into the soft dewy grass on his farm while she watched in horror.

"Tara. You're the prettiest blonde-haired, blue-eyed girl in Galesburg, Illinois, but you're also the most gullible. Nothing will happen to me because I smash some stupid toadstools, or whatever you call them." He strode toward the trees. "Let's see what we can find in the timber." He smirked and bounced his brows.

She frowned at him. He only wanted to find a secluded spot in the woods for another attempt to make out with her. When would he grow up and realize she didn't like him that way? She wasn't sure she liked him at all. Not after the last time he caught her alone in a stand of trees and wouldn't let her go. It was a blessing her brother's best friend Shane had come along. "You go on. I'm going home."

He turned and scowled. "I just got here, and you're leaving me?"

"I have enough wild daffodils for the dinner table. And I'm not in the mood for conversation." *At least not with an egotist.*

Tara sped to the edge of the Flynns' meadow between the house and thick trees. She'd forgotten to ask if he'd received his letter of acceptance to Yale next semester. He should have by now. Terry might know—although it had been a long time since Mac had hung out with her twin brother.

Over the past two years, Mac had become so strange. Always thinking of what *he* wanted and never anyone else. Never what he already had with his adoptive parents' enormous farm. He wasn't anything like Shane O'Leary.

Shane. She pictured his deep blue eyes and tousled, thick black hair. She'd been in love with him since their first year of high school.

And before that, puppy love, since the first time he'd hung out at the Flynn farm with Terry when they were little kids. He and Shane had become immediate best friends. Only natural since their farms were right next to each other. Shane told her she was his best friend too. Their close circle used to include Mac, but not anymore.

Tara breezed across the barnyard and through the back door into the kitchen of their white clapboard farmhouse.

"That's one fine-looking young man, Tara." Her mother pointed out the kitchen window toward the meadow. "Why didn't he come in?"

"Ah...he was passing by. He said he took the shortcut from town to their farm. And I didn't invite him."

Her mother turned toward her. "Why not, dear?"

Tara lifted a green vase from an overhead cabinet. She carried it to the table, slid into a chair, and arranged the daffodils. She sighed and faced her mother. "I didn't want to. Mac makes me uncomfortable." She couldn't tell her mother how many times he'd made passes at her. It would worry Mom. "He's all about himself. No one else and nothing else matters to him. All he talks about is leaving this *hick* town to move to the city and get rich when he graduates from college." She'd never fall in love with someone so self-centered.

"Remember when I told you about the fairy ring he destroyed on his farm last year? He didn't care that I loved those little circles in the field or about the risk he took. Nor that fairies were watching."

"Sweetie, I should never have allowed your grandmother to fill your head with those tales from the old country when she came to visit. This isn't Ireland. And there's nothing wrong with a young man trying to get ahead. Our family does well here on the farm, as do our neighbors, but Mac may not want a humble farmer's life."

"I'm glad Nanna told me those stories. They give me a sense of our heritage from Ireland. And I have everything I need right here on the farm."

Her mother squeezed Tara's shoulder and kissed her on the forehead.

After Easter dinner, Terry and Shane walked along the dirt road that led to the O'Leary farm. Terry picked up a stone and flung it at a tree on the other side of the ditch. "Received my acceptance from Yale. You?" He sure hoped Shane had. "I count on you to be my roommate."

"Yep. It came in the mail yesterday. I planned to tell you, but Dad and I worked until way after dark, and then it slipped my mind until bedtime. I'd have said something in church this morning, but you were in a conversation with your girlfriend." His eyes rolled skyward.

Terry laughed. "Man, that's a relief. Didn't relish the idea of a stranger for a roommate. What about Mac. Have you heard from him? It was a good idea for him to apply to Yale. They have a fantastic legal program. With his desire for a career in law, it's the place he needs to be."

"True. But nope, not a word. He's acted standoffish for the last couple of months. I meant to corner him and ask if I've done anything wrong, but I can't catch up with him. He's avoiding me." Shane shrugged.

"Same here." Terry furrowed his brows and nodded.

Two weeks later, Tara, Shane, and Terry were on their way back home after a night in town at the movies. Tara's heart did a flip when Shane latched onto her left hand.

He squeezed. "Tara, what made you choose Northwestern? With your grades, you could attend anywhere."

"It's close to home—an easy weekend trip when I get homesick. And Mom's been uptight. She worries that Dad's health isn't what it used to be. I can get my accounting degree and help out around here on weekends at the same time."

Terry stretched his arm across his sister's shoulders and squeezed. "Sure glad you'll handle the books and not me, sis."

She lunged at his foot with hers but missed.

"Seriously though," He moved out of her reach. "Mom and Dad will appreciate your being nearby. I will too. Dad gets tired much too fast. I'll take over the hard work this summer. And I've been rethinking my plan to go to Yale. Northwestern has a lot to offer besides being able to come home on weekends."

Shane leaned forward to see Terry. "Same here. Why go all the way to New York when Northwestern has what I need? And it's closer to home."

"This was all Mac's idea for you guys to move across the country." Tara huffed. "It's a prestigious school. One you'd want to graduate from if you studied law, but that's not what *you* want."

"Speaking of Mac..." Shane lowered his brows, "have either of you heard from him? Was he accepted to Yale?"

Terry scooped up a stone and skipped it down the road with his free hand. "Haven't heard a thing. You, Tara?"

"Not me." *Thank heavens.*

Shane joined the Flynns for dinner that night. Afterward, he and Terry took a walk along the country road between their family farms. Shane grew silent. Once they left for college, he'd only see Tara passing in the halls, on holidays, and during summer break.

"What's wrong?" Terry backed up the few steps he had taken after Shane stopped. "I'll bet I can guess. You're thinking of Tara."

Shane pictured her in his mind. Short curly mop of blonde hair, crystal blue eyes, full lips, and, like her twin brother, a hair shorter than him at his five feet, ten inches. "Yeah. With our heavy class schedules next fall, there won't be much time to get together."

"Have you asked her to the prom yet?"

"No."

"Man. You'd better get your act together before someone else asks her. Mac's been after her to go out with him forever. She has no interest in him, but if you continue to drag your feet, she might accept a date with him to the prom." He slapped Shane on the back, and they continued their walk.

"I'll do it as soon as we get back to your house. She sure was gorgeous in her purple dress last Sunday. It was hard to keep my mind on Pastor's sermon."

Terry punched him in the arm. "You've got it bad, fella."

Shane gave him a sheepish grin. "I've always had it bad for Tara."

The next week, Mac sidled up and sat next to Tara while she ate lunch on a bench outside the high school campus. *Oh, no.* She slid further away from him. He moved over, and Tara inched away again. If he came any closer, she'd fall off the bench. "Stop it, Mac."

He stared at her. "Once I get my law degree, I'll become a high-paid attorney. I'll be able to afford anything I want. And I won't come back to this hick town."

Tara's eyes narrowed. "Your family has more than most here in Galesburg, Mac," She'd never understand Mac's obsession with money or his desire to be *important.* "Your dad owns the largest feed store and runs the most prosperous farm. Don't you want to help him with his business?"

"That old flea-bitten place? Not on your life. I want something better."

Tara shook her head. "Whatever."

As he slipped his arm across the back of the bench, she stood and repositioned herself on the other end.

He frowned. "I guess Terry and Shane were accepted into Yale. Those guys didn't have any trouble with their grades. Straight-A students. But my grades aren't so bad either." He rose from the bench and stormed away.

What's that all about? Terry and Shane must not have told him they changed their minds and applied to Northwestern.

The day after high school graduation, Tara, Terry, and Shane had a picnic lunch in the meadow behind the Flynns' farm. She handed a sandwich to her brother and one to Shane. "Hope you guys like the lunch. I made the egg salad myself." She smiled at Shane. Her insides tickled each time his deep blue eyes focused on hers.

He took a mouthful, chewed, and swallowed. "Great sandwich." He grabbed a handful of chips from the bag she offered. "So...what did your grandmother tell you about the fairies on her last visit from Ireland?"

"Nanna said they're sometimes hard to understand." Tara took a sip of cola. "Most of the time, they live quiet, uneventful lives and simply observe humans. They prefer not to bother the *big people*, as they refer to us. I imagine they keep their distance because we're a strange bunch to them. Really, how many people do you know who've encountered one?"

"Don't mind her, Shane. Our grandmother has filled Tara's head with stories of fairies and leprechauns ever since she was born."

An apple flew through the air from her hands and hit Terry in the chest. "Stop it." Tara grabbed an orange and reared back.

He held his hands up, palms out. "Okay, okay. I surrender."

A chuckle came from Shane. "I've always been fascinated with fairies and leprechauns." He reached for more chips from the bag in the middle of their picnic blanket. "What else did your grandmother say about them?"

Tara gave her brother a smug expression, then turned to Shane. "Women fairies are heads of the clans." She took a bite of her sandwich, followed by a drink of cola. "I met a fairy one day."

As she chewed another mouthful of chips, her brother and Shane eyed each other.

Shane glanced at Tara. "You're pulling our legs."

"No. I'm not." She glared at her brother, whose shoulders shook from stifled laughter. "Do you want to hear this or not?"

Terry swept his hand in front of him. "You have the floor, sis."

"It happened a couple years ago when I was almost over the mumps." She shook her head at the unpleasant memory of the illness. "Being cooped up in the house all the time drove me nuts. Mom had gone into town. Dad was working in the barn. All of you were in school. I felt fine except for a little discomfort in my neck, so I decided to take a walk in the meadow. As I did, I thought about..." she peeked at Shane, and warmth flooded her cheeks, "...a few things. Before I realized what I was doing, I'd entered the thick stand of trees behind the barn."

"Sis, Mom warned us not to go into the woods alone."

"Yes, but with my thoughts so far away, I hadn't paid attention to where I walked." Her musings had traveled to the high school and Shane. "When I noticed where I was, I turned back. But I stopped when I heard beautiful singing. Light, airy voices. A glow further into the woods appeared. I hid behind a log to watch and listen for a minute, and the sound of the voices drew closer. Then they came into view."

Shane stared at her with rounded eyes. His jaw dropped. "What came into view? What did you see?"

"The fairies." The corners of her mouth rose. "Up until then, I thought Nanna had made up those stories from Ireland."

Her brother blew out a sharp breath and folded his arms over his stomach.

Shane fixed his eyes on hers. "Did you talk to them?"

The more Shane paid attention to her, the more heat radiated to her neck. She had to be beet red by now.

He leaned toward her. "Did they say anything to you?"

"No. I was too stunned to speak. They approached me, gave me a once-over, and continued on their way, deeper into the timbers. But as the group disappeared into a cloud of what resembled shiny dust, one female fairy turned back to me, waved, and disappeared too."

"Aww, hogwash. You have such an imagination, sis." Terry hopped up from the blanket, gathered his trash and the apple Tara had thrown at him, and headed to the house. "I'm gonna change and go swimming at the pond."

"Don't you want to join Terry?" She pulled her lips to one side and stared at Shane from under her lashes.

"Nah. I'd rather hear more about the fairies. Did you ever see them again?"

"Yes." Shane wouldn't rather swim with his best friend? Strange. He was full of surprises. As she gazed at him, he winked. A tingle skittered up her neck.

"When I left the woods, I strolled to the barn to see if Dad needed any help, but he wasn't there. I leaned on the loft ladder to wait for him, but instead of Dad, the female fairy showed up. She flew into the barn through a window and landed on the ladder one rung above me."

Shane's eyes grew rounder. "What happened next?"

"You're not going to say I made it up, or I'm crazy?"

"No. My grandmother spoke about the fairies in Ireland too. She'd seen them. Leprechauns too. But I was always more interested in fairies. Never knew they lived here. So, go ahead."

Might she and Shane have more in common than she'd ever thought? But Mom always said *opposites attract.*

"Well...the cute fairy, like the ones in children's books, glittery and glowing, settled on the rung and introduced herself. Her name is Athia. She was surprised I'd detected them. 'Most big people can't,' she said. 'There must be a reason you've been given the *gift*.'"

Shane's smile grew. "My mom said something similar happened to her once. The gift thing, I mean. I suppose she referred to the ability to see them."

"That's what I took it to mean, but I wonder why the gift came to me. Do you think it's because of the books I've read about fairies and elves?"

"Could be. Mom has a lot of fairy stories too. I should read more of them." He laughed. "What else did she say?"

"Athia talked for a long time. I forgot my lingering mumps, Dad, and where he'd gone. I was captivated by the tales about her grandmama, who was the head of their clan. She had warned Athia we big people have a variety of dispositions, some good, some not so good." Tara reached over and laid her hand on Shane's forearm. "Did you know fairies are so much alike, it's hard to tell them apart?"

Shane chuckled. "You mean the boys can't distinguish the difference between them and the girls? I find *that* hard to believe."

Tara hit him in his bicep and giggled. "No. She meant the fairies dispositions. She did say the male fairies were different from the females. Like us, except fairies have an iridescent glow, pointed ears, and wings. They're lovely. I wish you could see one."

"Me too. If they're as pretty as you." He leaned in and kissed her lips.

Her head spun. He'd never kissed her *that* way before.

Mac stood outside the dormitory at Northwestern. As soon as his parents had set up a checking account for him to use in college, he'd packed his bags and left Galesburg, planning to obtain a part-time job for extra spending money. Finally, away from the constant pushing for him to take over the farm and business. He'd had enough of the little hick town where he'd grown up. And of his folks' *guidance*.

He'd had enough of people asking him about Yale too. *Humph. Rejected.* As if he wasn't smart enough for them. Now he'd have to settle for this place.

Terry and Shane had decided not to go to Yale even though they'd been accepted. Why had they been accepted, and not him? "How stupid of them not to attend such a prestigious school," he said under his breath. Well, he'd better get settled in. At least Tara'd be here for his amusement.

A tall, shapely brunette sashayed by and smiled at Mac. His brows rose as he ogled her curves and the movement of her hips. *More amusement.*

Terry strode into Tara's bedroom. She'd try to talk him out of this for sure. "Tara, I've decided to stay home and take my classes online. With Dad's cancer diagnosis and declining health, he needs my help on the farm."

She ran across the room and hugged her brother. When she looked up, tears welled in her eyes. "I decided the same thing last night. Let's tell Mom and Dad. They've both been worried, but they didn't want to say anything."

Terry breathed a sigh of relief.

The siblings joined their parents in the kitchen. Tara took dishes out of the cabinet and set the table, while Terry lowered himself into the chair next to his father at the table. "Dad, we won't let anything happen to our farm. You and Mom don't have to be concerned over the chores while you go through chemotherapy. Tara and I decided to study online right here at home. Everything will be fine."

Dad's eyes glistened. "It's a blessing to have such caring children, willing to sacrifice for us. But what about the experiences you'll miss in college? I don't want to take those away from either of you."

After she'd turned off the stove, their mother placed the plate of pancakes on the table and wrapped her arms around her husband. A tear dropped to her cheek as she peered at her children. "Dad's right. Not everyone has the opportunity to go to Northwestern. We'll manage."

"No, Mom. I'm staying." She hugged her parents. "If millions of others can study online, we can too. You and Mom will be a help to us with your experience on the farm. We'll be the Flynn team." She beamed at her brother.

He'd always been proud of his sister, but not as much as now.

Their mother let loose her tears onto rosy pink cheeks. "How will you two manage classes and the farm? It's too much."

When Shane stopped by the house over the weekend, Tara and Terry told him their news. After they stepped into the living room and sat, Shane ran his fingers over Tara's soft cheek. Their decision didn't surprise him. "Mom told me your dad's bad news. Your mother needed someone to confide in. It's awesome that you're staying home to help out. Ever since I received my letter of acceptance from Northwestern, something has nagged me."

"What is it, Shane?" Her brows pinched.

Terry stood. "Before we have any more bad news, let's have the ice cream you mentioned earlier, sis." He led them into the kitchen.

Tara produced a gallon of mint chocolate chip ice cream from the freezer, while Terry took bowls out of the cabinet and put one in front of each of them at the table.

Shane chuckled. "We'll eat with our fingers?"

"Oh." Tara jumped up and retrieved three spoons from the utensil drawer.

"We'll dip it out with our fingers, right?" Terry glanced at his friend and guffawed.

Tara slapped the back of her brother's head. She grasped the ice cream scoop from another drawer. "Smart aleck! You could have helped." She returned to the table and lowered herself onto a chair.

"Yeah, I could have, but this was more fun." Terry laughed.

Shane stood. "Let me get the napkins." He crossed the room and brought back the napkin holder from the counter.

"Guess I'm not the best hostess." She pouted.

Before he retook his seat, Shane leaned over and kissed the top of her head. "You're the only hostess I need." *For the rest of my life.*

Tara's face turned a deep shade of pink. She peeked at her brother, who stifled his mirth.

He turned to Shane. "So, what's nagging at you, pal? Something we can help with?"

"Not really. I talked to Dad about Northwestern. The only reason I wanted to go there if both of you did was because it was my dad's alma mater. When I visited the feed store this morning, I ran into Pete Williams. He applied at Western Illinois University for the fall. They have a great agriculture program. And it's in McComb, only an hour away. Much better than a six-hour drive from Northwestern." He winked at Tara. "Pete said I still had time to apply. Why hadn't we considered it before?"

Terry shrugged. "Guess we were tied up in the hype from other students, especially Mac. I still can't figure out why I bothered with Yale."

Shane nodded. "If college life at Western doesn't work for me, I can take online classes like you two. Dad doesn't need me to work full-time on the farm with my three older brothers there, but I'd like to help."

Terry's lips formed a lopsided smile. "And you won't miss a certain someone since I'm sure you'll come home early on weekends and not have to go back so early."

As Shane watched Tara spoon out the ice cream into their bowls, her face deepened its color. His neck grew warm. "Can't let my girl get lonely. She might take up with one of these farm hicks in my absence."

Four years later

Shane tossed a bale of hay onto the wagon bed. "Tara, we've finished four long years of college at last."

"I know." She bit her lower lip. "After we decided to wait until we graduated to get married, I didn't think the time would ever get here. Mom and I already started the wedding plans...in our spare time." She tittered.

Shane grinned. "Good. Too bad your dad hasn't returned to his former robust self since the chemo. But I'm happy the treatment was successful. He'll be there to walk you down the aisle soon."

Tara checked her clipboard to see where they had to deliver the truckload of hay. She marked through the name, sauntered toward Shane, and wrapped her arms around him. "What I can't believe is how much work here you and Terry have finished these past four years. When you decided to do online studies from home for your last three years, things started hopping. This farm looks brand new with the repairs. Terry and Dad sure are grateful to you. I wasn't much use to them, except with the books. You truly are a godsend." She squeezed him again.

Mr. Flynn stepped into the barn. "Shane, at the risk of repeating myself, I appreciate your father allowing you to work for me, but I'm concerned you're needed on your dad's farm."

"Sir, my family gave their full blessing when I told them I wanted to help out here full-time. My folks care about your family. Besides..." his brows rose as he gave Tara's father a cockeyed smile, "...my brothers don't have me to trip over anymore. I feed them information on changes I think would be beneficial. They do the rest. And Mom and Dad were thrilled at the idea of my working here. Our families have been close as long as I can remember. They didn't want to see your farm go downhill."

Mr. Flynn shook his hand. "Your parents and I go back a very long way indeed. Guess we'll go even further, now that you and Tara will be married."

At dinner, Mr. and Mrs. Flynn told stories of how they and the O'Learys grew up together.

"Speaking of growing up together," Shane wiped his mouth with a napkin, "have you heard from Mac yet?" He glanced from Terry to Tara.

Across the table from Shane, Terry rose from his chair and quirked his mouth. "No. He sure has disappeared. Not one word in four years. Maybe he's moved on."

Several young women walked by as Mac leaned back on the campus bench. He'd enjoyed his years at Northwestern without his so-called *friends.* It had been a delight to make new ones. *Often.*

When the girls turned to him, he smiled and rose. Hadn't missed Tara much. Didn't miss the boring classes he'd have had to continue if he had decided to become a lawyer either. He'd made a wise decision to be a paralegal. After a few years, he might finish what he started. But, right now...he'd make new friends. "Hey, girls. Wait up."

In the wee hours of the next morning, Mac returned to the dorm. Those babes sure knew how to entertain a guy. He flopped onto his bed.

His most recent roommate, Chuck, stepped into the room in his jogging duds. "Hey, I thought you'd be gone by now."

"Cool your jets. I'm almost packed. Had to make a few last-minute *acquaintances* last night. You know how it is."

"No. I don't. You really think you're someone, Mac. Have you ever had more than a passing interest in a female? Glad my girlfriend went to another school. I would have hated to do something to you I'd regret later. Scratch that. There'd be no regret." He parked on his bed.

"My new roommate will move in today. Now I should be able to study for my masters without interruptions from your *visitors*. When will you leave?"

Mac rose from the bed and tossed a few final items into his suitcase from the desk drawer. He locked the luggage and placed it next to the door with his other bags. "Keep your shirt on. I have to admit you were a more tolerant roommate than the guys ahead of you. Thanks for not getting on my case...*too much.*" He snickered. "Time for me to say, *adios.*"

As Mac piled his bags together, he ground his teeth. He wouldn't make the money he hoped for as a paralegal. But becoming a lawyer required a much bigger commitment, both time and money. He had his bachelor's degree for now, and he didn't have to sweat the Law School Admission Test. There was no guarantee he'd be admitted either. Not with law schools as selective as they were.

He headed through the hall to the elevator. It would have been doubtful he'd graduate at the top of the class and get a job at a prestigious firm. Paralegal was enough for now. And he was a good one. Otherwise, his boss wouldn't have sent him to open an office for him.

Dragging his bags behind him in the twilight, he walked to the train. Over four years was a long time not to see or talk to Tara. He should have called her once in a while to keep her on the hook. But this way, it gave her more time to think about him, pine away for him.

Aboard the train, Mac settled into a seat and gazed out the window. He hit the speed dial number he'd reserved for Tara in high school. *Hope she hasn't changed it.* The phone rang. *Yes.*

"Hello?"

"Hi, sweet thing." The train jerked forward. "It's a pleasure to hear your voice." Mac smirked.

"Who is this?"

She didn't remember? He grimaced. "Tara, I'm hurt. You don't recognize me?"

"Mac?"

"Of course. I've missed you."

"Mac, I'm— "

"Sorry I haven't called in so long, but I'm coming home. Classes were brutal, but I graduated. Sure wish you'd have been there. Things were a blur with studying, graduation, and work. The ceremony came up so fast I didn't have time to invite anyone. Not even my parents were here." They hadn't bothered to call after he'd told them what he thought of their dominance over him. Always telling him what he should and shouldn't do. He sneered. "Anyway, I regretted not having you there."

"You're coming home? There's something I need to— "

"I've had second thoughts about leaving Galesburg. The town needs expert legal counsel. I'm opening an office." She'd never guess he wasn't a lawyer. Anyone who believed in fairies would believe anything he told her.

"That's wonderful, Mac, but I have something—"

"Say, could I get a lift from the train station since my folks don't live in town anymore? I can't wait to see you. The train's due in at noon. We'll have lunch."

A long sigh came through the phone. "Shane and Terry are in the fields, so I suppose I can pick you up. But you have to let me—"

"We'll have plenty of time to talk. Just the two of us. See you at noon." He disconnected the call.

Good thing his adoptive parents *had* moved away from Galesburg. Gave him the perfect excuse to ask Tara to give him a ride. They weren't his real parents anyway. More interested in themselves than him. Always had been. Guess he should be grateful they paid for school. Why had they? He looked out the window.

Still too dark to see anything out there. Might as well take a nap. He settled back in his seat. Shouldn't have stayed up all night, but those babes were worth it.

He rolled his head toward the dark window. He'd wanted to have Tara for a long time. He whispered to his reflection, "Soon, real soon." Whenever he'd caught her alone in the past, someone always interrupted and ruined his chance. Full lips and a swimsuit figure. "Man, she was well-endowed."

An uncomfortable sense that someone watched him swept over Mac. He turned to the wrinkled face of an elderly woman who occupied the seat next to him.

She glared.

A snigger escaped his lips. He ignored her and drifted back to his thoughts. Tara'd forgive his lack of attention. One side of his lips rose. He'd sweep her off her feet and plant his mouth over hers.

Tara lowered her cell phone to the dining room table and stared at it. She'd had no chance to tell him about her engagement to Shane. Typical Mac. Every conversation had to revolve around him. He wouldn't listen to anyone. "Like when I warned you not to step in the fairy ring."

Mac's parents had mentioned his rejection letter from Yale and how he decided not to become a lawyer. They'd been so disappointed when he'd gotten in trouble in Evanston for rowdy behavior, not to mention the girls' lives he'd ruined. That it was a joke to him was the worst part for Mr. and Mrs. Seaberg. No wonder they'd moved from Galesburg.

She finished her invoices on the computer and proceeded to the kitchen to make breakfast for the family. Her mother stood at the table, rolling dough for biscuits.

"Sit and enjoy your coffee, Mom. I'll do this."

"Sweetheart, you've done too much around here. I'll make breakfast this morning."

"Let's do it together." Tara took the rolling pin out of her mother's hands.

"Who was on the phone this early in the morning? Shane?"

"No, it was Mac Seaberg. After four years of silence."

Her mother's smile turned upside-down. "What did he want?"

"My...your response at his name sure has changed since our high school days, Mom." Tara raised her brows.

"Can you blame me after what his mother told me he'd been doing? Poor dear. I sure miss Clarisse. We were such close friends. I guess she needed someone to confide in."

"As you did me. But I'm glad you did."

"Yes, but Clarisse couldn't face anyone after that, and they left."

Tara patted her mother's back. She lifted the frying pan from the cabinet and took the eggs and bacon from the refrigerator. "He's turned into a real scoundrel."

"So, dear...what did young Mr. Seaberg want at this early hour? He didn't even know you'd be awake."

"He called to ask if I'd give him a lift from the train station at noon. He's coming home."

Her mother spun to her. "You're kidding."

"Nope."

"Why?"

"He said he's opening an office. You told me he'd changed his studies to become a paralegal, so I guess it's what he'll do. I didn't get a word in edgewise on the phone."

"So, you'll pick him up?" Her mother shook her head. "Will Shane go with you? Did you tell Mac you're engaged?"

"Shane's at work in the field. From my bedroom window, I watched him and Terry head out early. And in a few minutes, when they walk in, they'll be ravenous. So I'd better get the bacon on."

"I don't like the idea of you alone with Mac, even in the daytime. You didn't say if you told him you and Shane are engaged."

"Mom, I'll be fine. I can take care of myself. As I said, I hardly got a word in, so I haven't told him about our engagement...yet. But it's the first thing I'll inform him of when he steps off the train."

As the time neared afternoon, the antique clock on Tara's dresser struck once for the half-hour. She'd have less than an hour to get to the train station. Could Terry go in her place? Why hadn't she told her brother that Mac called? Because Terry would have insisted on going, and he had to get the rest of the potatoes harvested. He didn't need an interruption. Neither did Shane.

Not one word had she received from Mac in over four years. They'd not spoken very much before he'd left for college either. Tara grabbed her purse, flew through the hallway, and ran down the stairs to the living room.

How would Shane feel now that Mac had come home? He hadn't heard from his *supposed* friend either. She skipped down the front porch steps and slid behind the steering wheel of her Ford Escape.

"Shane always thinks the best of people." But she wasn't so sure Mac had a "*best*" in him anymore. She should have told him no.

From the train window, Mac searched the faces of the people who lined the platform. She hadn't come. The last day they'd actually spent talking on the farm played in his mind. He'd yelled to her. *"You'll jinx me with all this fairy ring garbage."* He hadn't meant it, but she didn't turn back on her way to the house. And the only time he'd spoken to her after that was after he'd received his rejection letter from Yale.

The train inched forward. Tara still wasn't in sight.

The car jerked to a stop, and the elderly woman next to him awoke with a start. She gathered her knitting basket and purse, stood, and shuffled down the aisle.

Mac snatched his briefcase and the small bag from under the seat. When he pulled his suitcase from the overhead compartment, it landed with a thud. He inched toward the end of the car with his bags.

He stepped from the train, surveyed the crowd once more, and spotted Tara at the far side of the station.

Mac jogged to her, charcoal-gray bags rolling behind him. He reached for the back of Tara's head and pulled her toward him, but she turned her face away. His lips landed on her cheek. "It's great to see you. You look fantastic."

She'd filled out more than he remembered. In all the right places. *Very alluring.*

Tara pulled away from him. "Hi, Mac. It's been a long time." She led him in silence to the parking lot and opened the trunk.

"Thanks for picking me up, *sweet thing*." He threw his bags in.

"Sure. But please do not refer to me that way. And why call me after no word for how long? I have something to tell you."

Tara slipped into the driver's seat. Mac lowered himself across from her. Before she started the engine, he laid his hand on her arm. "Aw, c'mon, Tara. You have no idea how exhausting studying the law is."

"But while you were away—"

"So now I'm back, and we can get *reacquainted*." He leaned forward, his lips aimed toward her neck.

She pulled away. "Stop it, Mac. Will you let me tell you my news?"

"What could be more important than talking about us, sweet thing?"

She pushed him toward the other side of the car. "You're no more observant than you were in high school. I'm engaged." She flashed her engagement ring in front of him.

"Engaged to who?" Not that it mattered to him. He wouldn't care if she were married. He wanted her even more now. The thought of how easy it'd be to take her away from someone else amused him. He ogled her until she glared.

"Shane proposed before we started our first year of college. We've waited until after graduation to get married. Our wedding plans are set for Christmas."

Shane. Mac fumed.

A few weeks went by. Mac had settled into his apartment and started his duties at the office, but he still hadn't gotten anywhere with Tara. She'd avoided him in town and every time he visited the farm on the pretense of *seeing his buddies*.

"I have to think of something." His intense desire for her drove him crazy. Thoughts burned in him at night. How would he get her alone? Maybe he should marry her. These farm girls were big on pleasing their men. And he'd make sure she understood what *pleased* him—after they were married. But how could he get her to call off her present engagement?

Hmm. Tara's twenty-third birthday would be soon. He'd call Shane and ask to help with a surprise party for her. The naïve jerk might go for it. Now to figure out a way to get rid of Shane and have it appear he'd run out on Tara.

Mac made the call. "Say, Shane. Can you meet me for lunch today? I have a suggestion for a surprise birthday party for Tara."

A couple of hours later, as the men polished off their burgers at the local diner, Shane held out his hand to Mac. "I wouldn't have come up with anything this unique on my own. She'll love a barn dance. Meet me for dinner at the steak house tonight, after my co-op meeting, and we'll finish the details. Tara's having dinner with the girls she chose for bridesmaids, so she'll be none the wiser."

Mac's insides were giddy. Soon, he'd have Tara all to himself.

Shane downed his cola and wiped his mouth with the napkin. "You've taken on a lot for someone who's been out of our lives for so long, Mac. You're *sure* you want to do this?"

"Not a problem, *Buddy.*"

At dinner that night, Shane gritted his teeth. He'd been told Mac was up to no good. Had it been a dream? Shane shook his head. He had to believe the rest of the warnings were real. The scoundrel intended to do away with his competition and convince Tara the engagement was off. Mac had no idea how disappointed Tara had been when he'd returned to Galesburg.

As Mac ate the rest of his dinner in silence, Shane glanced at him and visualized the wheels turning in the man's head. The way he'd stared at Tara every time she came into view, touched her. It had been noticed. *And by more than me.*

"Mac, why don't you come over to the Flynns' house for dessert? I promised Tara's mother I'd save room. Terry, his folks, and I plan to watch a little TV tonight until Tara comes home. If it's not too late for you. She made a pound cake last night. It's still your favorite, isn't it? She should be back from her girls-night-out by the time we finish."

A smirk covered Mac's face. "Love pound cake. No. Not too late at all."

"We can leave your car in the parking lot." Shane smiled. "I'll drive you back here later this evening to retrieve it."

"Sure, why not?"

When they arrived at the Flynns' farm, Shane pulled his truck behind the barn. They got out, but before they rounded the structure, Shane stopped. "Hey, before we go in, I thought of something else for Tara's birthday party. Let's take a hike in the field and discuss it, so she won't see us *plotting* if she shows up early."

"Sure. What did you have in mind?"

The two men walked into the field and skirted the woods where Shane and Tara had seen a fairy ring earlier that day.

"Mac, did you know Tara loves Irish music? She loves everything Irish. You should remember how she told us back in high school about the Irish fairies and fairy rings."

"Yeah, I remember. What if I find a Celtic band to play at the party? Irish is popular now. Shouldn't be hard to find one."

Mac spun toward the farmhouse. "Let's go back."

"She's not home yet." Shane tightened his jaw. "Girls lose track of time when they have fun. Let's walk a little farther. There's something you need to see."

When they'd reached the halfway mark in the meadow, Shane pointed to a ring of mushrooms in their path. "Remember these?"

"Ah. A stupid mushroom ring. Haven't stomped one for a while." Mac stepped into the ring. "Look at me. I'm in danger." He snickered, spun, and waved his arms in the air. In a flash, he vanished.

"*Humph!* So, you thought you'd have Tara for yourself and take advantage of her, did you? My *old friend*? You never listened to anyone. Same old Mac. You should have believed her."

Shane pursed his lips. "I wonder where they took you."

Mac slumbered as visions came into his head. He watched himself step into the fairy ring, dance like a crazed leprechaun, and smash the delicate mushrooms. The tinkling sound of wind chimes came to his ears. A girl watched from outside the ring.

His eyes slowly opened, and he focused on the vision before him. Trees and bushes turned pale, pastel shapes twirled in clouds like an approaching storm. Sparkling crystals of snow formed and joined the colored clouds in a swirl. A bright snowy light surrounded the girl.

As he floated into the air, unclear visions of faces with fragile features and wispy white hair came closer. Beings with transparent, glowing wings danced in circles around him. The ground below disappeared. His eyelids grew heavy again. He closed them.

Shane continued toward the house. The faint music of wind chimes sounded in the field behind him. He turned to observe the sun drop below the horizon. Sparkling lights and glittering dust wafted on the gentle evening breeze. A moment later, the lights faded. Shane smiled. "Mac, I'd feel guilty about what I've done if you weren't such a scoundrel. But I had to protect my Tara."

As Shane rounded the front corner of the Flynns' house, Tara drove into the farmyard. He ran to meet her. "Sweetheart, I have a confession to make."

Tara turned her head and stared at him from the sides of her eyes. "What kind of confession? Tell me you didn't read my diary again like you and Terry did when we were teens."

He clamped his lips together. "No, but I kind of wish it was only that. Although...I did find it *interesting* reading." His brows rose. "When I read you loved me as much as I loved you."

She slapped his arm. "So confess already."

Shane led her to the front porch swing and sat beside her. "Mac's gone."

"What do you mean he's gone? As in moved away?"

Taking her hands in his, he bowed his head. "For the past couple of weeks, it occurred to me that Mac intended to steal you away from me. Not sure what he'd planned, but it wasn't good. Pete Williams, who's been living in the apartment next to Mac, said Mac was bad news. One night Mac was drunk and told Pete he intended to have you for himself. All he had to do was eliminate me."

The evening grew darker as Shane disclosed his meeting with Mac and the party plans. "It was a ruse. He'd planned my demise. So, I had to disrupt his scheme."

Tara stroked Shane's stubbled chin. "I've had an uneasy sense about Mac since he came back home. The way he leered at me. The things he said. But what did you do?"

"Remember the stories you told us about the fairy rings? And how Mac always scoffed at you?"

"Yes, he said I was a fool to believe in such things. He would never listen to reason. He never believed one thing I told him, much less listened to the warnings."

"He believes now."

"What do you mean?" Her forehead wrinkled with questions.

"For the past few nights, a voice came to me while asleep. At first, I thought it was dreams, but there were no visions—only a voice. A soft melodic voice spoke in my ear and warned me about Mac. I recalled you saying fairies watched over us. One night, the voice told me Mac planned to get rid of me in the woods behind your farm. Another night, it said Mac planned to convince you of his love. And when I was gone, he'd make you think I'd run off."

Tara shook her head. "Shane. I've had similar dreams...I mean a voice told me things. It said I was in danger, and so were you."

Shane nodded.

"I believed they were nightmares. My imagination ran wild because of Mac's *touchy-feely* actions when he'd come over. He was really getting to me."

"He can't *get* to you anymore. In any way."

She grabbed his arm. "Why? What happened?"

"I led him into the meadow and showed him the fairy ring we found this morning. Just as I thought he would, he hopped into the middle of it and crushed the mushrooms. He danced in the circle...until he vanished."

Her eyes grew round. Her hand flew to her mouth. "*Oh.*"

"Oh, yes."

Tara laughed.

"Tara, Mac's gone." Shane frowned. "I'm not sure what'll happen to him now, and it's my fault. I can't help but feel guilty, even if Mac had become a reprobate."

She rested her forehead against Shane's chest as she continued to chortle. When she straightened, tears trickled onto her cheeks. "It's okay, Honey. This isn't your fault, it's Mac's. And no harm will come to him. It's probably the best thing that could have happened to him, considering the direction in life he'd chosen, and the pain he'd caused others."

"I don't understand."

"Last week, when Nanna came to visit, she told us more fairy and leprechaun folklore. She said fairies are gentlefolk, not given to pranks and mischievous behavior as are the leprechauns. Fairies try to help humans when they need it. She'd been told by one of her fairy friends they'd removed a lad from her town in Ireland. Someone who caused trouble for others." She rested her head on Shane's shoulder.

"Nanna said the fairies grew rings throughout the town to catch the lad. They waited for him to set foot in one, and when he did, they whisked him away." Tara giggled.

Shane's jaw dropped. "Is what she said true? I mean, I know Mac was taken away because I witnessed it happen. But what about the helping part?"

"Nanna's fairy friend told her they often whisper warnings in the ears of humans, so they can be forewarned of danger. And when the fairies capture a human, they take them back in time. They cause them to grow younger and younger until they're babies again. Nanna says it's something in their voices when in the fairy realm. They deliver the baby to a couple who needs a child. The lad they took from her town has a chance to start a new life and become a better man. And so does Mac...now."

Shane took in a deep breath and blew. He held Tara in his arms. "Thank you. With each step I took away from the fairy ring, my heart grew heavier. You've lifted the weight." He covered her lips with his.

Mac opened his eyes and gazed at the beautiful creature before him. He'd never seen anything like her before. Light shone through and around her. He was blinded to everything except her delicate white tendrils of hair and iridescent wings. His mouth dropped open. This was no dream. Where was he? *Who* was he?

As she spoke, Mac forgot his questions. His body was numb and yet tingly at the same time.

The exquisite creature took him by the hand and led him away. Where was she taking him? The way ahead was filled with pinpricks of light and a faraway glow.

"You must not let riches of this world spoil you as you have in the past. Remember, it's easy to lose integrity if you are not careful. Pay close attention, young man. It will help you in the future."

Athia led the young man to a moss-covered log. "Sit here and relax."

Mac leaned against the wood. He slid his hands across the moss on either side of him. So soft. As he stretched out on the green carpet, his eyes grew heavy.

Athia peered at the child resting on a bed of soft green moss. He grew younger while she watched. A smile formed on his cherub-like lips. "Sleep on, my lad. You should have listened to Miss Tara when she told you what she'd learned about fairies and fairy rings."

The fairy sprinkled Mac with more fairy dust as he slept.

"One should never enter a fairy ring on purpose, especially not to destroy. They might find themselves whisked away to...*where* is not important. She warned you. But you ignored her. Not a nice thing for a young man to do."

Athia watched him slumber. She continued to speak with tinkling words of wisdom, and Mac grew younger...and younger...and younger...

The End

Keep thy heart with all diligence; for out of it are the issues of life. Proverbs 4:23

Email Date
@

Email Date

Genre: Women's Fiction

After graduation from college, Denise and her friends take a trip to Pensacola, Florida, before launching into their careers. A vacation to remember for the rest of their lives. But something unexpected happens to one of them on the trip.

Email Date

Where had the last four years gone? Denise Kelly's gaze landed on her best friends, Alexandria Kennedy and Jodie Knight. They'd been best friends forever. Would they all go their separate ways? What would life be like without them nearby every day?

Denise drew in a deep breath and surveyed the rest of the graduation class that filled the halls as they waited for the commencement ceremony to begin.

Her two friends came closer. The decision to attend the University of Alabama in Birmingham together had come naturally. What a great time they'd had, despite their academic struggles. She sighed. Here they were, about to pass another milestone. *Graduation.*

The three girls pulled each other into a group hug.

Denise smoothed her shoulder-length, brunette locks in place, adjusted her cap, and straightened her gown. She linked her arms with her friends. They marched to the commencement line. "This is it. Soon we'll have to buckle down to our careers."

"But first," Alexandria's blue-gray eyes sparkled in the fluorescent lights of the hall, "I plan to enjoy summer on the beach. Can't wait to wear my new bikini." She whisked her waist-length blonde hair behind her and raised her brows.

As one side of Jodie's lips rose, Denise could imagine what she was thinking. Jodie had always been insecure about her tomboyish figure when the three of them had gone to the pool. As hard as Denise tried, she couldn't convince Jodie she looked fine in a bathing suit.

Denise bumped Jodie with her elbow and smiled. "With that royal purple, one-piece you bought last week on our summer wear shopping excursion, people will assume you're a swimsuit model. Very attractive on you."

Jodie returned her smile and shrugged. "If you say so."

The organist played the first notes to *Pomp and Circumstance*, the graduates scurried to their places in line, and the commencement ceremony began. As the line moved forward, Alexandria let out a soft squeal. "I'm so glad each of our last names starts with a K. Kelly, Kennedy, and Knight." She snatched a hand of each of them and thrust them into the air. "Together, all the way, now and forever."

Alexandria, the dramatist. Denise laughed. But in two months, Alexandria would be off to New York to pursue her dream of becoming a professional violinist. They wouldn't all be together anymore. *Don't let it spoil the day.* She'd mess up her makeup with tears, and Mom and Dad were ready to take pictures as she descended the stage.

"Denise Kelly..."

As the faculty member read off her accomplishments, Denise made her way to the platform and shook hands with the dean, who handed her a diploma. She turned and headed for the stairs on the other side of the stage.

Alexandria's name was announced while Denise's parents snapped pictures of their daughter descending the stairs.

"Jodie Knight..."

Ah, Jodie. She'd been so worried about college, but she'd finished with top grades. Next stop for her, more studies. Once Jodie had realized she wanted to be a pediatrician during her second year, her plans blossomed. What a revelation she'd had. And with her love for children, she'd be a good one. Her sweet disposition, soft brown eyes and hair, and melodious voice would relax her young patients. But she'd be too busy to keep in touch for the next four years, even though she'd still be here in Birmingham.

Oh, bother. Here come the tears, and there's Mom with the camera.

Hugs, best wishes, and kisses followed the ceremony. Next came the graduation party at the Kelly's home on Double Oak Lake outside Birmingham. The three girls stole away to the backyard, which overlooked the water.

Denise swallowed a mouthful of chocolate cake with raspberry filling and chocolate ganache frosting. "Before we begin serious life—"

"Ha!" Jodie blew her bangs upward and grimaced. "As if four years of college weren't serious enough?"

"Now, let me finish, girl." Denise chuckled at her all-too-*serious* friend. "You especially need to relax a little. I meant the business of moving ahead in our careers. You're on your way to becoming a respected pediatrician. Alexandria is headed to New York with her violin. And I," she glanced at her fingernails, polished them against her shoulder, and grinned, "start work at the local museum in September. My dream job. But, for the next two or three weeks, I want to relax and have a bit of fun."

Jodie pursed her lips. "I suppose you're all for that, Miss Poster Child for blonde jokes."

Alexandria feigned shock at the comment, but giggles broke out. "I have a degree, you know."

Denise almost choked on her cola. "You two just never quit, do you?"

The girls chortled and finished their cake.

"So, what did you have in mind, Denise?" Alexandria collected their plates and placed them on the glass-top rolling cart next to the patio table.

"What do you say we pool our finances and take a trip to Pensacola, Florida? The Gulf Coast. Sugar-white sandy beaches. Emerald green water. Or so the ads say. I did my research when I considered West Florida University in Pensacola instead of Birmingham." Loyalty to her friends had won out over the lure of four years in a vacation/resort town setting. But her friends were worth it.

"Our new bathing suits are perfect for Pensacola." Denise leaned back in the chair. "This'll be an adventure we'll remember for the rest of our lives."

"Wow, take a gander at that surf. Listen to it. And look at those plants waving in the breeze. It looks like a wheat field. I think those are called sea oats if I remember right." Denise grabbed her suitcase from the trunk of her car and placed it on a luggage cart. "We'll wake up to this every morning for the next ten days. Let's hurry and check-in. Then we can hit the beach until dinnertime."

Alexandria hauled out her three suitcases. "Did you see all those guys out there?"

Jodie yanked her one bag from the bottom of the trunk. "Alex, I can't believe you brought three huge pieces of luggage for only ten days. Really?"

"I intend to appear at my best." Alexandria raised her chin. "You never know who I might meet."

The girls registered at the front desk and strolled to their room.

As Jodie tossed her single suitcase onto the dresser, Denise stifled a laugh at the dissimilarities in the three of them. They had disagreed over a lot of things through the years but somehow remained best friends. Like sisters from different parents.

"Where should we eat tonight after we lounge around on that beautiful sand?" Denise pointed her thumb out the picture window toward the Gulf.

"On the beach?" Alexandria had her nose pressed to the glass as three bronzed, musclebound men tossed a football to each other along the water's edge.

Jodie rolled her eyes and hung up her dresses. She laid her shorts, tops, and lingerie in a bottom dresser drawer. "There, that should leave enough room for you two. I vote for fast food."

"I used two drawers." Denise held her hand out toward Alexandria. "That leaves six for you."

The blonde tossed a stuffed suitcase on top of a bed. "You're both jealous. Or have low expectations. I brought everything from my new bikini to a gown...just in case."

"A formal?" Jodie planted her hands on her hips. "Girl, people who come to Pensacola for vacation don't plan to go to places where you dress fancy."

Denise shook her head. "From what I've read, people dress casually here, for the most part. This is one big sand dune."

Alexandria pouted. "Well, I didn't know. But, maybe I'll run into a native or two, who'll invite me to a big shindig." She plopped onto the bed.

Jodie's lips tugged to one side. "You're as likely to see a native Pensacolean wearing formal attire as you are to see an Eskimo in this semi-tropical paradise. Denise told us this is a laid-back community."

Lowering herself to the bed, Denise stretched her arm around Alexandria's shoulder. "Cheer up. As you said, you never know what will happen in the next ten days on this barrier island."

After a shower to wash off the Gulf's salt water, Denise stepped out of the bathroom in her robe. "Girls, we still haven't decided where to go for dinner tonight." She rubbed her hair with a towel. "And I don't want fast food when we have amazing options for local cuisine."

Jodie pulled on the laces of her canvas shoes. "How about that place down the road? The one with the pirate name. Oh, what was it?

Captain Jack's? No, that was the guy in the swashbuckler movie we watched the other night."

"You mean Peg Leg Pete's?" Alexandria's brows rose. She lifted one side of her lips. "That would be my choice." She spun and faced Jodie. "Will wonders never cease? We agree on something for a change."

Denise chortled. "It's settled then. Peg Leg's it is."

Alexandria slipped into a mauve sundress with a tiny flowered pattern around the skirt's flared hem and sparkles around the scooped neckline.

"Aren't you a little overdressed for the occasion?" Jodie stared at Alexandria through her long dark lashes.

The blonde shrugged, twirled, and snatched her sequined purse. "What will you wear, Denise?"

"I think jeans and my 'I love history' T-shirt will do. But you look fantastic. You, too, Jodie. The white pedal pushers and beige peasant blouse are perfect on you. You may snag a pirate in that garb."

Jodie's brows shot upward. "With Miss Glamour Puss along? I doubt it. All eyes will be on her. And if not her, you with your curvaceous figure and dazzling green eyes. They say brunettes are the women men marry...like you. I'm doomed."

They laughed until tears welled in their eyes.

"Jodie, your day will come. But who'd want me? An academic? We're going for food, not to catch a husband. Let's get out of here before the dinner rush starts."

Birmingham
Four years later

Denise smiled and sipped her coffee as she gazed around the restaurant. Never thought she'd see an establishment such as this open in her old stomping grounds. With a room so much like Peg Leg Pete's in Pensacola. Uncanny. Scenes from the vacation she, Jodie, and Alexandria had taken after college graduation flashed through her mind. One particular incident tickled her.

It was wonderful to share an evening with her old friends whom she hadn't talked to for more than three years. Each of their lives had gotten so busy they drifted apart. Her news might shock them. But she hoped they'd be happy for her.

"Doesn't this place remind you of something?" Alexandria, still the cute, petite blonde after three years of marriage and two children, turned in her seat to look behind her.

Denise gave her a thumbs-up. "Exactly what I thought."

From her chair between them, Jodie gave the room a once-over. "Remind us of what?"

"Oh, Jodie...look." Alexandria nodded her head toward a waiter. "Don't you remember? Pensacola, a few years ago. That guy who was so attracted to me at the restaurant?"

The glare Jodie gave would have reduced an ice sculpture to a puddle had one stood between the two girls.

Jodie blew a quick puff of air between her lips. "I remember the restaurant as similar to this one, but not any guy who drooled over *you*."

"The place brings back fond memories," Denise added. "Same rustic décor and fishing boat paraphernalia on the walls. Yes, *very* fond memories."

"Yeah, but this stuff doesn't appear used..." Alexandria scrunched her nose, "...like in Pensacola. Barnacles and broken shells embedded in the wood of an old rowboat as though they had dragged it up from the bottom of the Gulf."

Jodie lifted a menu from a rack in the middle of the table. "The décor in Pensacola may have been rustic, but the restaurant was clean. And the guy you referred to had his eye on Denise, not you."

"So, what shall we order for lunch, ladies?" Denise grabbed two menus and handed one to Alexandria. *I had no idea you noticed, Jodie.*

"That was a nice trip," Denise recalled after a waiter with brown hair had taken their orders. "I found the forts fascinating, as well as the tour of West Florida University."

"Who cares about forts and schools? Did you see his eyes? Green as emeralds like yours, Denise. He's gorgeous! And he sure reminds me of the one in Pensacola."

Denise chuckled. She remembered his eyes. *And how could I ever forget when he slid that note under my plate?* As she bit her lip, her face grew warm.

"Poor Alex." Jodie patted the petite blonde's back. "You tried so hard to get his attention. I remember how you flirted with him when you handed him the tip instead of leaving it on the table. And to leave him your cell phone number? You *were* determined."

"Well, who could blame me?" Alexandria giggled. "It was brazen of me. But I'm past that now. And content to be the wife of a fellow violinist."

"And we're happy for you." Jodie placed a napkin on her lap, though their food had not yet arrived.

As Alexandria inquired about Jodie's future possibilities of marriage, considering the multitude of doctors she worked with, Denise lost herself in memories of the Pensacola trip.

When the waiter placed her food in front of her back then, she was shocked to find an envelope under the plate. A corner of the paper peeked out at her. She slipped it into her purse while her friends argued over who had a more enjoyable day on the beach.

Denise had excused herself and hurried to the restroom where she read the note. Her thoughts raced that day. The improbability of such a handsome man writing her that note when Alexandria had paid so much attention to him had puzzled her for days. *Sometimes it still did.*

The message played in her mind. *My name is Paul. I'm the assistant manager, filling in tonight for one of our waiters. Although house rules say we shouldn't get personal with our guests, when I saw you bow your head in prayer, I had to meet you. Judging by your conversation with your friends, you must be a visitor to Pensacola. Sorry if I eavesdropped, but I'd like to get to know you. Please email me. 1legalbeagel@yahoo*

Denise had chuckled for days over the email address, but her heartbeat had gone into overdrive. Both excitement and fear gripped her.

Alexandria returned the conversation to Peg Leg Pete's restaurant and the waiter. She frowned. "I sure made a fool of myself that day with that hunk."

During dessert, the blonde again brought up their trip to Pensacola.

"Now tell me he doesn't resemble the Adonis at the pirate place." She glanced at the man three tables away, taking a customer's order. "He's got the same wavy brown hair—"

"No, Alex." Jodie grimaced at her. "Your memory is so bad, it makes me wonder how you remember the notes to play. The guy in Florida had sandy-blond hair."

They were both wrong. Denise stifled a laugh. Auburn, with a military haircut.

"Well, he's the same height and build," Alexandria insisted.

Denise took a sip of water. Wrong again. *Paul's at least four inches taller than this man.* Water almost spewed from her mouth as her friends stared each other down. She covered her lips with a napkin, trying to hold her laughter in.

"Alex, that waiter we saw on vacation was much heavier than this one. What do you think, Denise?"

Before she could answer, Alexandria spoke up again. "I'll bet his magnetic green eyes sparkle just like the guy's in Pensacola."

Paul does have sparkling green eyes that hold your gaze like magnets. The corners of Denise's lips turned upward.

"Okay." Jodie craned her neck. "Here comes our food. Enough with the Adonis you thought you had on your hook four years ago...but didn't."

"Yes, let's pray over the meal and then move on." Denise nodded. "I want to hear what's transpired in your lives since we parted ways back then."

So busy reminiscing, they still hadn't noticed she wore a wedding ring. Denise laid her left hand next to her plate and drummed her fingers.

After Jodie said the blessing, the girls dove into their hamburgers and fries.

Denise swallowed. "So, what else has happened in your life, Alexandria? Besides the symphony, marriage, and two beautiful children?"

Alexandria gave them a rundown of the past three years after her wedding. Her gaze never once set on Denise's hand. Jodie's account was next. She ended her story with the description of a doctor she'd started to date a month ago.

"Your turn, Denise." Jodie held her hand out as if she'd introduced her to an audience.

Some audience they were. Not very attentive. Denise removed her hand from the table and exhaled a puff of air. "As you'll recall, I moved to Pensacola to work at a local museum several months after our visit there."

"I remember." Alexandria pointed her fork at Denise. "That's when I lost touch with you. I was so frenzied with our concert schedule. Sure am glad you found me again on Facebook last month though."

"I'm sorry I didn't write to either of you. But things were hectic. I knew neither of you could get away to Pensacola then for the wedding and—"

"*Wedding!*" Jodie lowered her forkful of fries to her plate.

"Yes. And, I remember that waiter from Peg Leg Pete's in Pensacola *quite* well." She raised her brows and waved her left hand in front of them. "I wake him up every morning for breakfast. Paul was the assistant manager of Peg Leg Pete's while he worked toward his law degree. We emailed each other daily for several months before I moved to Pensacola to plan our beach wedding. We moved to Birmingham last year when he started his own practice. My green-eyed, auburn-haired, six-foot, four-inch hunk of a man is a lawyer now."

Her friends' mouths dropped open as she flashed her impressive heart-shaped diamond ring set in front of them. "You didn't even notice." She laid her hand on her slightly rounded abdomen. "Paul Junior is due in about five months."

The End

Trust in the Lord with all thine heart; and lean not unto thine own understanding. In all thy ways acknowledge him, and he shall direct thy paths. Proverbs 3:5, 6

Overdue

Overdue

Genre: Romance

While author, Chad Dunbar, seeks help for his writer's block at the library, he encounters a gorgeous woman who stabs his finger with her long nail in an attempt to grab the same book he has aimed for. After she tears up, he lets her have the only copy of the book and finds another. But is this the end of their story?

Overdue

If something didn't change, his writing career was doomed. Chad Dunbar strode through the door to the library on the Lone Star College campus. A young man with curly brown hair, wearing earbuds and reminding Chad of himself in high school, bumped into him.

Chad stepped aside. "Sorry. Should watch where I'm walking."

The student lowered the cell phone he'd been staring at, looked up with his dark brown eyes identical to Chad's, and gave him a thumbs-up, then breezed through the exit.

Spooky seeing himself as a teen, but the kid should have been the one watching where *he* was going. Chad shook his head. Man, he'd been in a foul mood all morning. Two weeks to the deadline for his historical mystery. Would he make it? What he needed was a new agent. Bill had become too demanding. Downright pushy.

The nonfiction area was just ahead. He had to find something to help him with a dynamic climax to his story. What about that book on writing prompts to add fireworks to scenes? *Drat.* What was the title? He couldn't remember the author either. If this didn't make him the ultimate numbskull, he didn't know what would.

Chad entered the aisle and perused the volumes along one side. Nothing caught his attention until he glimpsed a tall blonde entering from the other end. She strolled behind him, leaving the scent of jasmine in her wake. *Hmmm.* Cute. He clenched his teeth and snapped his head back to face the shelves. *Concentrate.* The blonde drifted a few feet from him.

Why had this paralyzing writer's block struck now? He'd never experienced difficulty coming up with ideas before. Something about writing techniques might jumpstart his imagination. Nothing else had worked, not even the multitude of online sites for writers he'd visited.

He pulled out a book on the basics of writing. Too *technical.* He stifled a laugh. But then...he *was* desperate. Maybe he should go back to the beginning. Nah. He returned the paperback to the shelf.

As he closed the distance between himself and the blonde, he spotted an interesting title, *Research Techniques for Historical Romance*. Now that might be a mind-jogger. The combination of mystery and unrequited love had worked for him in the past. He lunged for the lone copy on the top shelf.

Before he could wrap his hand around it, pink nails gouged his skin. "Ow!" Chad jerked his hand back. He cradled the stinging paw to his chest as his eyes shot daggers at the woman. But at the sight of her sparkling green eyes surrounded by thick, dark lashes, his fiery darts fell to the floor.

His attacker's eyes rounded. She backed away. Wheat-colored waves swept across her shoulders and ended in a soft upward curl. "Sorry. You're not bleeding, are you?"

A smoldering fire flared inside him again as he inspected his finger. "No. And it's still attached to my hand." This day was going from bad to worse.

"I'm very sorry. I noticed the hardcopy of *Research Techniques* up there—were you after the same book?"

Chad's eyes locked onto hers. His mouth opened. He pressed his lips together and took a deep breath. *Stop gawking.* "I was until you stabbed me. I've been searching for...information for a story I'm writing."

"Oh, so you're a writer?"

"Yes."

"So am I." She gazed at the volume still on the top shelf.

He couldn't afford the distraction of a beautiful woman at a time like this. The last thing he wanted. He should grab the book and leave.

The blonde smiled again and repeated. "So. You're a writer."

"Ye-e-es?"

Her eyes narrowed. "And you need *that*?" She pointed to the top shelf.

Chad's brows rose. He lifted his hand and latched onto the hardcover. When he brought it down, she reached to take it from him. He moved an arms-length away from her.

Her mouth formed a pout. "But I need it for the historical romance I'm writing. I have a deadline to meet, and there's only one copy."

"Look, lady. I'm an author with a demanding agent who insists I turn in a new historical mystery in less time than I have to do a good job." He took a breath. "I need it more than you. Find something else." *That* was rude. His lips pulled to one side. He hadn't meant to be uncouth.

"Well, excuse me. What makes your story more important than mine?" She crossed her arms and cocked her head.

Chad stifled a chuckle. Was that a spark of fire he'd seen flash in her eyes? Must be Irish. Her crystal green orbs intrigued him. There was something familiar about her. Had they met somewhere? Her face softened, and her eyes moistened.

No. Not tears.

His willpower faltered at the weepy-eyed woman. *You're weak.* He pursed his lips. "Okay. You're right. If it's that important, here."

She held out her palm.

As he placed the book in it, his fingers grazed her warm, soft skin.

She yanked her hand back as if she'd received an electrical shock. The book dropped to the floor.

He bent to pick it up and his head collided with hers. They straightened. Rubbing his forehead, he handed the hardback to her. "Sorry."

The lady author smoothed her hair back and rubbed the red circle near her temple. "Thank you. As soon as I finish, I'll bring it back. I won't renew it. And you can reserve it, you know. That way, you'll get it right away."

"Yeah. Sure. Unless someone else has it on reserve." He touched the welt rising on his forehead and winced. "It's all right. I'll find something else."

She propped her hand on her hip. "If it was on reserve, it wouldn't have been on the shelf. Quite the martyr, aren't you?"

Chad tugged his lips to one side. "I don't have time to wait. I'll find another resource."

The blonde grimaced and walked away. As she neared the end of the aisle, she stopped, glanced at him, and flipped open the book cover.

He turned to the shelves and renewed his search. The beautiful young woman remained at the entrance of the aisle, perusing the pages. Why didn't she leave? *Focus on finding the help you need, dummy.*

As he ran his index finger across several titles, one caught his attention, *The Ins and Outs of Historical Research*. This might do. A few new methods would come in handy since he'd exhausted everything he knew to do so far. Maybe he'd find a technique that would trigger something for the mystery. Chad took the hardback from the shelf and opened it. "It'll work."

When he checked the aisle, she'd gone. He let out a sigh of relief. No more distraction. As he left the nonfiction section, he flipped through the first few pages. A note from the author caught his eye, distracting him as he walked. He came to a sudden stop as he collided with a body.

"He-e-ey." Green eyes glared at him. "Not you again. Why don't you watch what you're doing?"

Great! "Me? You stabbed me with those daggers of yours, remember?" Her gorgeous features and emerald eyes planted themselves in his mind. He didn't need this. He didn't want it. Not at the moment. Not when his career depended on him staying concentrated on his writing.

The person in front of her left, and the perfectly proportioned Venus turned, stepped to the counter, and laid down the book with her library card on top of it.

A twenty-something-year-old red-haired female with a name badge that read Jenny Longstadt, Student Librarian, continued a heated conversation on her cell phone, oblivious to Miss Author.

As she ended the call with an audible huff, a young man wearing a similar plastic name tag to Jenny's approached. Red's face looked like she had sucked on a kosher dill for breakfast.

The young man rested his hand on Red's arm. "Bad news, Jenny?"

"That two-timing boyfriend of mine canceled his last date with me. I've had it."

"Best news I've had all day." The male smirked. "Now you can go to the party with me tonight."

The lady author's eyes closed, and her head fell backward. She stared at the ceiling for a second and then back at the couple behind the desk. Miss Author drummed a long pink nail on her card.

Jenny eyed the tapping finger and then the woman. "Sorry to keep you." The student librarian seized the book and laid it to her left. She picked up the card and examined it.

Chad tapped his foot on the tiled floor. *Come on.* He had to get home and work on his story.

The male librarian turned to him. "I'll take care of you over here." Chad shifted to his right, dropped the hardcopy on the counter, and read the guy's nametag. Alan Willoughby. "Thanks, Alan."

The young man set the research volume between him and Red, on top of Miss Author's book. Alan scanned the card Chad gave him and waited for the computer to process the information. Alan bumped Jenny's arm. "So-o-o. Will you go to the party with me?"

Jenny's cheeks turned crimson. "I'm not sure. Where is it?"

He turned and leaned toward her.

Miss Author resumed her nail tapping, this time on the wooden counter.

Without turning his head, Chad peeked at her. The blonde's eyes widened, and her nostrils flared. Her lips pressed together. He'd better do something, or she'd blow.

His hand slapped down on the counter. "Ahem."

Alan jerked his attention away from Jenny. "Yes?"

"Do you think you two could postpone your personal agendas until this lady and I have our reading materials and can leave you to your *private* conversation, in which we have no interest?"

While the student librarians glowered, Jenny stuck the book in a plastic library bag and handed it to Miss Author. Alan did the same, shoving the other bag at Chad.

The stunning female author spun, gave Chad a nod, and headed for the exit. Over her shoulder, she said, "Thanks."

He snatched his bag and stomped out of the building.

Chad arrived home and rushed inside, ready to buckle down to work. Hercules, his black Great Dane, dashed into the foyer to greet his human. "Hey, fella. I know, I know. You need to go out, pronto." He tossed the book bag on the couch and raced Herc to the door to let him into the backyard.

While Hercules attended to business outside, Chad built a ham sandwich and brewed a pot of coffee. He needed the caffeine to energize him.

Minutes later, he entered the living room juggling the sandwich, a pile of nacho chips smothered in salsa, and the steaming mug. When he'd settled himself on the couch with his food on the end table, he stretched across the cushions and reached for the library bag from the other end. "Hope this cures my inability to finish this story."

Chad opened the sack and wrapped his fingers around its treasure. Something wasn't right. *Odd.* He thought the book was larger than this.

As he drew out the hardback copy, his jaw slackened. He hopped up from the couch. *Research Techniques for Historical Romance.* "The Casanova librarian gave me the wrong book." He fisted his right hand and jerked his elbow backward. *Vindicated!*

The book fell to the floor with a thud. Chad retrieved it and ran his hand over the cover. He took in a deep breath and exhaled. The author lady with the dazzling eyes would be furious when she found her bag didn't hold what she wanted. He gritted his teeth. He'd have to give the book back.

Herc scratched at the back door. "What? Oh, yeah. You want in." Chad hurried from the living room, through the kitchen, and opened the back door. His four-legged buddy bounded into the house and went straight for the ham sandwich on the end table, Chad right on his tail.

"Oh no, you don't, big guy. This is mine." He snatched the plate. "Stay. I'll get you a treat."

He took his lunch into the kitchen, placed it on the table, and dug a dog biscuit out of the jar on the counter.

"Woof!" The Dane was right behind him.

Chad shook his head at the dog. "Sit, Herc." This time, the dog obeyed. Chad gave him his treat. "Obedience training for you was a waste of time and money, my friend. Now, what was I doing? Oh, yeah." What an idiot he'd been. He hadn't asked the blonde for her name. Otherwise, it'd be easy to look her up online. No doubt, she'd have an author page on Facebook or Twitter. But, without the name—

He paced from the kitchen to the living room and back. Herc joined him. "Thanks for the company, boy." Chad dropped into a chair and ran his hand down the dog's neck.

After a bite of the sandwich, he chewed on the situation. He'd have to go back to the library, explain to the librarians what happened, and obtain her information from them. Not sure they'd give it though. "Herc, I'm in trouble."

The dog's dark chocolate eyes stared at him. He cocked his head, and a whine, which sounded more like a question, came out. Herc opened and closed his mouth.

"What are you trying to say, Herc?" If only his buddy could talk, he might offer words of wisdom in this dilemma. Chad scratched the dog's ears and let out a guffaw. Sure, he would. "Boy, I met the most attractive woman I've ever seen. Then I decided I didn't need a distraction in my life right now. Can you believe it?" The dog whined again.

"And she's a writer too."

Herc cocked his head the other way as if thinking, "What?"

"I have no idea who she is. Oh, well, she hates me by now anyway. I didn't present myself as much of a gentleman."

A mournful howl came out of the Dane. He landed a front paw on Chad's leg.

Chad patted the paw. "My sentiments exactly, pal."

Was there any way to correct this mess? "The only thing I can do is go back to the library and work on my story there. She's sure to show since I have the book she wants."

"Arf!"

"You'll be okay in the backyard for the rest of the afternoon, won't you, Herc?"

"R-r-ruff."

"Good. I'll fill your water pail."

Chad took care of the dog and left the house. No telling how long he'd have to wait for her to show up again. Hope he hadn't missed her.

He jumped into his deep red King Ranch pickup and sped to the library.

When Chad strode up to Jenny behind the checkout desk, her eyes widened. She pulled her lips to one side. "And what can I do for you *now...sir?*"

Attitude? She's giving me attitude? He laid *Research Techniques for Historical Romance* on the counter and pinned her with his gaze. "Alan gave me the wrong book earlier. And you gave the young woman you were helping the one I needed. You and your admirer were paying more attention to each other than your duties."

She glared at the hardcover. Her face turned a shade of deep rose.

Chad lowered his hand to the top of the volume. "May I have the lady's name, so I can give this to her?"

The girl's eyes grew larger. "I can't divulge that to you. Let me have the book, and I'll give it to her when she returns."

"Yeah. Right. What about *mine*?" He grabbed the romance book and turned. It was worth a try.

"Aren't you going to leave it here for her?"

As he walked away, he shook his head.

Chad found a seat facing the entrance at a table near the front of the library. He took out his notebook and opened the book. May as well take advantage while he had it in his possession. He ran his finger down the first page.

Around dinnertime, he called his neighbor and explained where he was. "I'm afraid I can't leave yet. Would you mind checking on Herc?"

"Not at all, Chad. I'll bring him over to our house, feed him, and keep him until you get home."

By closing time, Chad had written a ton of notes for the perfect climax to his story. He surveyed the library and blew a breath between his lips. Guess he'd try tomorrow to catch his lady author.

He packed his things into the library bag and glanced around the room one last time. Everyone had left except him. The guard at the entrance glowered and crossed his arms. Chad shouldered his bag and headed for the door. "Sorry, man. Didn't realize how late it was."

As he reached the parking lot, a shiny orange BMW convertible pulled away from the building. *"It's her."* He sprinted to the curb. "Hey, stop!" The BMW turned onto the street. The driver's long blonde hair waved as she accelerated. Either she hadn't seen him...or she'd ignored him.

Lady-writer must have a day job that prevented her from coming earlier, and she tried to get here before closing but realized it was too late. He'd have to come back tomorrow before noon in case she dropped by during her lunch break. If she didn't show, he'd have to stay later.

He chuckled as he jogged to his truck. She drove the same way he did. And in the BMW he'd checked out a few months ago at the dealership. Same color. Metallic sunset orange. Sure was a beauty. He grimaced. His lifestyle demanded a truck, not a fancy puddle jumper. He'd never get Herc and their camping equipment in that tiny thing.

"Sa-a-ay." A weekend of camping was just the ticket to relax his nerves. They'd been cooped up for the past couple of months with the story. Same four walls. No wonder his creativity had been blocked.

Chad bounced into the cab and cranked the engine. He shifted into gear and drove toward home. After he returned this book to the other author, he and Herc would get away to the mountains where he could concentrate. He'd get his mind off her and back onto his writing.

The next day, Chad arrived at the library an hour before noon. He chose the same table and started in on his work. While he typed, he kept a vigilant watch for the lady author.

Three hours later, he peered at the wall clock. Two o'clock. He'd finished a first draft of his story's climax, thanks to the book mix-up. Proved handy. He should buy a copy for his home library.

He cupped his chin in his hand, elbow on the table, and observed the entrance. No blonde writer, so far. Did he dare leave and come back later? Better not take the chance. She needed to get her manuscript done too. He'd grab something at the coffee shop here in the library. With its see-through walls, he could still monitor the doors. Chad stuffed everything in his backpack and strolled into the shop.

At a table next to the glass partition, he savored the black coffee and cinnamon roll. An hour later, his stomach growled again. He'd have to deal with it. He ensconced himself once more at the table near the entry. Good thing he'd asked the neighbor to let Herc out for him while he was stuck here.

Several hours passed. The guard squinted at him. Chad scanned the area. He was the only one left...again. He threw his things together, exited the library, and stood on the sidewalk at the edge of the curb searching for the BMW. *Not here. I don't understand.* He thought she needed this book.

As he trudged to his truck to drive home, Chad clenched his teeth. Yet another day at the library tomorrow. She'd better show. At least he was getting the work done.

As Chad sat at breakfast the next morning, his thoughts niggled. What if she was in an accident? *Or kidnapped?* He pressed his eyelids closed. His imagination had gotten out of hand. They weren't characters in one of his historical mysteries.

Hmmm. But they could be. Not a bad idea. "Herc, I may use this weird experience with the striking creature from the library for a whole new story." He scribbled a few notes onto a notepad, then checked his watch. "This should be the last day I leave you to yourself. Be nice to the neighbor. She's doing us both a favor by taking care of you for me."

He snatched the sack lunch he'd prepared and rushed out the door.

The day the books came due, Chad readied himself for his day at the library. Why had he wasted all this time waiting for this gal when she *obviously* didn't care he had the book she wanted so desperately? At least he'd finished his story, and it was now in Bill's happy hands.

Herc blinked at Chad with sad eyes. "Sorry, fella. One more day at the library."

The dog gave a pitiful whine and lowered himself to the floor, head resting on his paws. Two big chocolate eyes peered upward.

"Hey, Herc. What if I bring you a special treat when I get home? Will it make up for the neglect?"

Herc leaped to attention. His tail whipped back and forth so fast, it was a blur. Chad laughed. "Okay, buddy. Special treat it is." He scratched Herc's ears and grabbed his backpack with the library book inside. How did that dog know what he'd said to him? He'd never understand it.

As he locked the door behind him, his thoughts drifted to the beautiful blonde author. For sure, she'd show up today. He'd get to the library as the doors opened, and—he hit his forehead with his palm. *Blockhead!* He never checked the bookshelf to see if she'd returned it. Never asked about it either.

Chad sprang over the hedge between his driveway and the neighbor's, then ran up the porch steps to the front door. He rang the doorbell and listened as it played *The Yellow Rose of Texas.* Mrs. Ryan answered in her typical denim jeans and a T-shirt, with her youngest son, Bobby, clinging to her leg. By the disheveled hair, he guessed she'd had a rough morning. No time for grooming.

"Good morning, Chad. What brings you to our door so early?"

"Hate to bother you at this time in the morning, Barb, but I need another favor." He dangled the spare keys to his house in front of her. "I have to spend one last day at the library...ah...to finish my story. Would you mind taking care of him one more time? The big guy's afraid of thunder, which is in the forecast, so he may need a little more attention." Chad furrowed his brows. "He's already depressed because I've left him alone so much."

"Sure. No problem." She took the key and looked down at her son. "Want to check on Hercules with me again? I'm sure he'd like someone to play with." The boy nodded and hid behind his mother.

"Thanks, Barb. Thanks, Bobby. Herc loves to play with us guys."

The grin on Bobby's cherub face almost covered it and showed every tooth in his mouth.

Chad spun, cleared the three steps from the porch to the sidewalk, and turned. "Bobby, take good care of my buddy."

Barb and her son giggled as Chad hurried toward his truck. He slid into the cab and drove away.

At the library, Chad rushed to the shelf where he'd originally found the book he thought he'd checked out. Not there. He claimed his place at the table in front of the entry and planted himself. Guess she'd decided to use it for her writing since she didn't have this one. All this time waiting for her. What was he doing? *Ha!* He knew precisely what he was doing. It wasn't simply to return the book either. He wanted to see her again.

He kept an eye on the return slot in the wall inside the doors, as well as the one outside the entrance. If he had a nickel for every returned novel, he'd be rich. Bet she wouldn't get there until closing time, or even after hours. He wasn't staying through the night.

After the library closed, Chad called Barb. "Sorry, I'm so late. I've run into an unavoidable delay. I'll make it up to you guys."

"No problem. Bobby had a ball today with Hercules, and I was able to read a book I've been meaning to finish for the last month. It was good for us to chill out for a while. We'll go back over and let him out again. And the rains never came, so Bobby can run out in the back with him. He loves your dog."

Chad thanked her and ended the call.

Two hours later, he still waited in his truck. "Man, what a waste of time." Except for finishing the story. The only thing left for him to do now was wait to hear Bill's confirmation that the story was good to go. At least he'd made his agent happy again.

Chad checked the parking lot. His was the last vehicle. *Where could she be?*

He turned the key, and the truck engine roared to life. As he drove toward the street, his previous uneasy thought nagged at him. Had something happened to her? Was there a way to find out? The librarians might cave and give him her name if he begged. Or offered a bribe? He'd say it was a matter of life or death...or his career, though that was no longer an issue. And since *The Ins and Outs of Historical Research* was now overdue—

He slammed on the brakes. "*Idiot.*" He stared at *Research Techniques for Historical Romance* lying in the passenger seat. "You forgot to turn in the one you have." He zoomed back to the entrance, hopped out of the cab, and slid the hardback into the return slot.

As he headed back to the truck, he kicked a stone. *Let it go, man.* How? He had to know she was all right. Why? He didn't know her. But he wanted to. Guess tomorrow would bring yet another day at the library. *Ugh.*

Chad pulled into the driveway, hurtled over the hedges between the yards, and moseyed up the stairs to the Ryans' front door. Barbara's husband swung it open before Chad had a chance to knock.

"Hi, Al."

"Hey, neighbor. Barb said you had to spend the day at the library *again*. Isn't this a little late for a writer to be cramming?" Al chuckled.

"You have no clue."

"Come on in. I'll get your key."

"Actually, I thought I'd ask Barb...and Bobby," Chad smiled, "if they'd mind checking on Herc tomorrow too. What I need at the library...um...I haven't accomplished my task yet. I hope it'll only take one more day."

"I'm sure they'll be happy to check on him, but you'd better ask her yourself. She may have something planned for tomorrow she hasn't told me yet. You know how it is."

Chad followed Al down the hall to the family room. No, he didn't know. He'd never had a wife, and he'd been too busy for a long-term girlfriend. So far, he'd only shared his life with Herc. He'd devoted his heart to his writing. *Up until now.*

Barb sat on the floor with their three children, arms spread out and intertwined like they were playing Twister as they worked a huge jigsaw puzzle. She glanced at him as he entered. "Hi, Chad. Join us."

"Thanks, but I'm beat."

"You want your key." She stood.

"No. It's a spare. I thought I'd ask if you and Al could hang onto it for emergencies. Barb, would it be too much trouble to take care of Herc for me one more day?" If Miss Author didn't show up tomorrow, he'd had enough. "I have to go back to the library. Last time, I promise. Not sure how late I'll be."

Barb sank back to the floor. "Not at all. You're sure tied up in research for this story, aren't you?"

"You might say that." He lifted one side of his lips into a cockeyed grin. "Well, I need to get something to eat, feed Herc, and call it a night. Thanks for the help. See you tomorrow."

Al clapped his hand on Chad's shoulder. "Hey, why don't you have dinner with us tomorrow? It's our usual Friday pizza-and-movie night."

The rest of the family chimed in with pleas for him to say yes. Barb hushed the children. "Kids, please. Let the man answer." She peered up at him. "We're having a few friends over to make a small party of it. Al set up the big-screen television on the enclosed patio, and we'll barbeque too. We'd love to have you join us."

The corners of Chad's mouth turned up. Perfect. Exactly what he needed to get lady author off his mind. "Sure. What can I bring?"

Al shook his head. "Nothing but yourself. I've tasted your cooking." He snorted.

The Ryans had been wonderful neighbors ever since they moved in last year. He hadn't paid enough attention to them or their kids. Time for a change. He could write and still have a life. He should start a story about the Ryans. They were a real hoot at times. "I meant from the store, pal. Sodas? Chips? Desserts? Anything?" The men headed for the front door.

"Like I said, just you. Barb has everything under control."

She rushed down the hall to them. "Wait, Chad. Since it's so late, here's your dinner. We had a ton of leftovers tonight—mac and cheese casserole, and I slipped in a couple crescents." She handed him a grocery sack with two plastic containers in it.

"Thanks, Barb. Beats P B and J hands down. You're a lifesaver."

She giggled and returned to the kitchen.

"You have a sweet girl there, Al."

"Yeah. I know. You need to find one of those for yourself, man."

"Someday." Would Al's sister Grace be at their party tomorrow? He'd met her a few months ago. Stunning woman. Almost as gorgeous as—*quit*.

Chad trudged out the front door and down the steps. Could he stop thinking about the woman writer, or her beautiful face, around a houseful of married people? Marriage. With his desire bent on becoming a successful author, he'd not given marriage a thought. Why on earth was it on his mind? He didn't know the blonde's name, much less anything else about her. What had happened to him? Over a book.

The next day, Chad sat at his usual post in the library, self-editing another story. He hoped he hadn't missed any problems with the timeline while watching for Miss Historical Romance Writer at the same time. If he had, it'd be her fault. *Yeah, right.*

As dinner time approached, Chad packed up his laptop with a heavy heart. The entire situation had become ridiculous. Was she a figment of his imagination? He inspected his hand. No, she was real. The pain from her fingernail-stab replayed in his thoughts, though she'd left no permanent mark. He needed to get his mind *off* this woman. Tonight, he'd devote his attention to the Ryan kids. Time for some fun.

Chad strode out of the library. He'd had enough of this place to last him a long time. After this experience, he might not visit another library for the rest of his life. He trudged to his truck, climbed in, and started the engine. As he drove out of the parking spot, he gave the entrance one last scan. There she was, dropping a book into the overnight return slot.

It had to be the one *swifty-Alan* should have given him—overdue now. He didn't care if it was only a small charge for the fee. She'd better pay it.

"Matter of fact—I'll tell her so."

He spun his vehicle and sped toward the building's entrance. The BMW had left, crossed the lot, and entered the street. Chad rocketed the truck around parked cars, across empty spaces, and turned onto the boulevard in the same direction. *Can't let her get away again.* If he honked, it might scare her. He'd catch her at a stoplight.

After several blocks, the BMW slowed for a red light. Before she'd come to a stop, the confounded thing turned green again. *Drat.* Even the lights were against him.

At the next intersection, a sudden rush of vehicles cut off his line of sight to her car. "Now where'd she go?" *Stupid drivers.*

When the traffic cleared, the BMW had disappeared. "You've got to be kidding me." So close. He slammed his fist on the steering wheel. Chad pulled over and hung his head. He frowned. Oh well, what did it matter? The books were returned, his story finished. He might see her again at the library someday. Or not. "Time to move on."

Chad turned the next corner and headed home. Besides, for all he knew, she was married. He hadn't checked for a wedding ring the day she stabbed him. He'd been too busy marveling at those amazing emerald green eyes, long blonde hair, and beguiling face. Well, her figure, too, but not the ring finger. He chuckled. He'd find her profile picture on the back of a novel someday. "So long, Miss Historical Romance Writer." *It's been quite the adventure.*

As Chad rolled into his driveway, Al jogged over to him. Herc barked from the Ryans' fenced yard. "Hey, man. Glad you're home. The food'll be ready soon. We brought Hercules over here, so he could play with the kids."

Chad slid out of the truck. "Thanks. Hear that, Herc? You've been invited to your first party."

"Ruff."

The men laughed.

Chad grabbed his backpack from the passenger seat. "Let me drop off my gear and freshen up. I'll be over in a few."

After a shower, he dressed in his best jeans and a cowboy shirt, yanked on his boots, and combed his hair. He grasped Herc's red bandana from the foyer table. As he stepped out to the front porch, his stomach growled. The aroma of grilled bratwurst and burgers wafted through the air. Excited clatter came from next door. The party was in full force.

From the back seat of his truck, he grabbed the sack of drinks and chips he'd bought on the way home and headed to the Ryans'. The kids met him at their front door with Herc. Chad slipped the red bandanna over the dog's head. "There you go. Now, you're dressed for a party."

Al came up the hall and took the grocery bag from Chad. "Hey. Told you to just bring you."

"Well, I figured the kids would enjoy a little junk food. Did your sister, Grace, come tonight?"

"Nah. She had a date. But I'll bet she'll regret it when I tell her you joined us. Outside of you, she'd have been the only single among us. That's probably why she didn't want to come." They entered the kitchen.

Chad followed him through the enclosed patio to the backyard, where the grill filled the air with more tantalizing aromas. "Onions, peppers, potatoes, hot dogs...ribs too? What happened to pizza?"

Al flipped the burgers. "These won't take long. Since everyone we invited said they were coming, except for my sister, we decided to go all out."

The doorbell chimed *The Yellow Rose of Texas.* Barb called from the living room, "Must be the pizzas. I'll get them."

A few minutes later, she carried a stack of pizza boxes to the folding table set up in the enclosed patio. "Al, look who I found behind the pizza boy?"

Chad moved inside to help Barb. A woman with blonde hair came up behind her. His jaw dropped.

Al hung the tongs on the grill handle, zoomed inside to the blonde, and captured her in a hug. "Emily, I thought you said you were too busy with your story to make it to your brother's little party."

Chad closed his mouth.

An alluring smile spread across Emily's face. When she turned in his direction, the beam in her emerald eyes disappeared. *"You."*

Al whipped his head around to Chad. "You?"

Barb wedged herself between Emily and her husband and stared at Chad with wide eyes. "You're the one?" She slapped her hand over her lips as her shoulders shook.

Chad's head was spinning. "*Me*? I'm *what* one? Did I miss something?"

Al stifled a laugh. "Em told us about the incident at the library. We didn't know it was at Lone Star or that it involved you."

Chad turned to Emily. "When I came home, I discovered I had the wrong book. I tried to find out who you were. *That mix-up* wasn't my fault."

He jerked his head toward Al and pinched his brows together. "Your sister? You have *two* sisters?"

"Yep. Almost identical, except for the shade and length of hair, and being a year apart." Al grinned.

Emily focused on Chad, then her brother. "And he's the neighbor you said I had to meet?"

"Yep." His grin grew wider.

She glared at Chad. "So, you didn't bother to check the title until you arrived home, huh? Convenient. My brother built you up as a nice guy. A *gentleman* wouldn't steal the book a lady needed."

No wonder she'd seemed familiar when he first met her. She and Grace did resemble one another. "Look, Emily. How was I supposed to know the student librarians were incompetent? But then, you didn't either, did you?"

As Emily's face glowed pink, a blue Great Dane trotted through the back door and sat at her feet. The dog studied him with her dark blue eyes. Emily stroked the dog's sleek coat.

Chad's mouth opened again. "Wow, a blue Dane. Beautiful. Is she yours?"

"Yes. This is Thena."

"Thena? Odd name."

"It's short for *A*-thena." Her eyes shot daggers. "Do you have a problem with it?"

Chad lost himself in the flicker of fire in her green eyes. Then they softened. He mentally shook his mind clear. "No. No problem. I have a Dane too." He pointed out toward the backyard where Herc bolted after a thrown stick. "His name is Hercules. Small world, huh?" A Cheshire cat smile spread across his face.

Emily chortled. "Seems so." She turned her attention to Herc. "He's so black, like midnight."

"Yeah. He's a beaut. Thought about getting a blue to keep Herc company, but haven't had time to find one." He held out his hand to her. "Chad Dunbar. If I'd been in my right mind the day we met, I would have introduced myself and found out your name."

Emily placed her soft, dainty hand in his. A huge sparkling diamond ring adorned it.

Chad's shoulders slumped. She was engaged. *Wait.* That was her right hand. He glanced at her left, where it rested on Thena's neck. *Bare*. Nothing sparkled but the blue's rhinestone collar. His insides heated.

"Chad Dunbar? I've read a few interviews on you. You appear different from your picture though."

"I use an old one. Too busy to have a new professional pic taken." An awkward silence filled the space between them. "So, Miss Emily. Do you have a last name?"

She narrowed her eyes. "It's *Ryan*."

He chuckled. "Of course. Guess my head's still not together."

She slid her hand out of his grip as they both glanced around them. Barb fidgeted with the table. Al flipped burgers and hotdogs on the grill. The other guests busied themselves in conversation.

Chad gazed back into her emerald green eyes. "Tell me. Were you able to get your writing done without *Research Techniques for Historical Romance*? And again, I'm sorry you didn't have it. I waited for you in the library every day to give it to you."

"You were there? Every day? I stopped by a couple of times but didn't see you, so I gave up. I have to admit...I was upset. It's a good thing I didn't see you. As it turns out, I did get the story written with the assistance of the book you chose. It turned out to be an immense help, and I'm afraid I turned the book in late. But, my agent is pleased with the manuscript. She says it'll be another bestseller."

"You were there? In the mornings, right?"

She nodded.

"I had the timing figured wrong. Thought I saw you in a BMW the first evening. I ran to the curb and waved, but it kept going."

"An orange BMW?"

"Yes."

"It was me. I was on the way home from a meeting with my agent. I stopped to get your name from the librarian but realized they wouldn't give me personal information, so I left. Did you get the research you needed?"

Chad nodded. "I finished the story, and my agent says it's a winner. Wait a minute. Your agent said yours would be *another* bestseller. You already have one?"

"I have two."

Chad's brows furrowed. "I've never heard of Emily Ryan."

"No, you won't. I write under the name of Emma O'Neill."

"Emma O'Neill? I've read your work. Guess I've never paid attention to the picture on the back cover."

The Ryan children squealed as they raced through the yard with the black Dane on their heels barking and howling. Thena yipped. Emily walked to the screen door of the enclosed patio and turned. "Does Hercules play well with other dogs?"

"One hundred percent better than his master does with other writers." Chad laughed and joined her.

She opened the screen door and let the blue Dane out. "Go show him what the kids love, Thena." The dog bounded off to join the Ryan siblings and Herc.

After the usual canine greetings, the children and two dogs began a game of hide-and-seek. Chad turned to Emily. "If you'll agree to compare notes on writing over dinner with me tomorrow evening, I won't charge you the overdue fee." He grinned. "Just the two of us?"

Her dazzling smile reappeared, sending a tingle into Chad's heart.

"I'd love to. Historical romance and historical mystery might be a good combination." She pressed her lips together. A delicate shade of pink colored her face.

One side of his lips tugged upward. Were those wedding bells ringing in his head? The library book wasn't the only thing *overdue*.

He'd need no help with romantic research on this story...as long as he had a willing partner.

Emily peeked at him from under her dark, lush lashes. Her eyes twinkled.

Judging by the way she looked at him, she'd be willing. *Emily Dunbar.* It had a nice ring to it.

The End

To every thing there is a season, and a time to every purpose under the heaven: Ecclesiastes 3:1

My Little
Friend

My Little Friend

Genre: Fable

A very special teapot travels from England to America and learns a lesson about selflessness and kindness.

My Little Friend

Hello. My name is Old Country Roses Royal Albert. My friend Faith says I'm not her usual type of friend. That's because I'm a teapot. Yes, it's a long name, but my friends call me OCRRA for short. It's pronounced O-kra.

You'll hear more about my friend Faith further into the story, but for now...

I was born in England in a factory. Before I knew it, I'd been wrapped up tight and stuffed into a box.

Not long after the traumatic experience of being placed in the dark for days on end, I found myself jostled about for...well, can't say how long either of those occurrences took place. You see, I can't tell time.

When the jostling stopped, the box lid slowly opened, and a beam of light struck me. The next thing I knew, someone lifted me out of the box, turned me over, and inspected my bottom. *How rude!* Many people stood around me and smiled. One big man, all dressed in black and white, called them staff. Later I found out they worked in an impressive place by the name of Buckingham Palace. It sounded very important to me.

The staff said I'd be presented to a queen as her birthday gift. My belly swelled with pride. *A queen. Imagine that.*

Back in the box I went. More jostling ensued. When it stopped, I rested for a long time.

One day, I awoke to being jostled about again. Muffled voices sounded excited...and hurried. Box and all, I was carried some distance and left to sit once more. This time not for long.

After people sang a merry song and cheered, the beam of light entered the box again. Gentle, warm hands lifted me out, then oohed and aahed over me. A lovely white-haired lady with a band of sparkles on her head held me up and smiled. She said, "You're perfect."

While other people in the room made comments, I marveled at my surroundings. Everything was so elegant. Nothing like the place where I'd come to life.

Wow! This is my home?

Months after I came to live in the palace with the queen, the maids rushed in to dust my special place of honor in the Queen's Palace Suite.

"Sally, did you hear? Her Majesty is to have a guest from America."

"I did, Gail. 'Tis the lady who has written to her for several years. Her last letter said she would be coming to London. The queen sent her an invitation to the palace so she could meet the author of such elegant words, as Herself said."

Late one afternoon, a lady with light brown hair and hazel eyes entered the room. Her Majesty ordered tea while I observed from my display case.

The man referred to as the footman, although he doesn't have anything to do with feet, took me out of the cabinet and handed me to a maid. "Her Majesty has requested her favorite teapot be used in the tea service."

Oh, boy, something new to do.

I was given a bath in a tub with some bubbly stuff that tickled and then a shower to get rid of the bubbles. Leaves the maids called Earl Grey were dropped inside me. Next came a bellyful of steaming water. *Oh... so warm, and what a delicious aroma.* The cook placed something called a "cozy" on me. It was like a pillow with an opening in one side with just enough room to go over and around me. My porcelain skin grew warmer as I was lifted onto a silver tray and carried away.

When the maid removed the cozy, I found myself back in the Queen's Palace Suite with Her Majesty and the nice lady named Ida. *I* was the center of attention.

But as the lady continued to gaze at me, tears flooded her eyes and slid down her cheeks.

"What is the matter, my dear? Why do you cry?" My queen reached for the lady's hand.

I was alarmed too. I'd never made anyone cry before, and I couldn't ask what I'd done to upset her. All I could do was wish the lady's tears away.

"Your Majesty, forgive me. The roses on this dear teapot remind me of those gorgeous blooms my late husband used to bring to me from his garden. I've always loved the combination of gold, pink, and deep rose-colored flowers. Andrew grew rose bushes for me and picked a bouquet every day in season. When he passed away, the bushes never bloomed again."

The queen gave her a handkerchief, and the lady dabbed at her eyes.

My gracious queen smiled and patted the lady's hand. She offered words of comfort, and soon they shared happy memories of days gone by.

Her Majesty had me bathed again and packed securely in my original box at the end of their tea party.

As the lady prepared to leave the palace, my queen presented me to her, and their voices drifted into my box. "I want you to have my favorite teapot as a token of friendship between us and to remember those beautiful roses your loving husband used to give you. Promise you will not cry when you see the flowers. Smile instead at the love he showed when he brought them to you."

Safely tucked away in the box, I left Her Majesty. I had mixed feelings about leaving Buckingham Palace and the queen. But as my new friend Ida carried me with her, I pondered what had happened.

The queen had done something selfless for someone else. Her tone of voice told me it made her happy. That made me happy, and my new friend had stopped her tears.

Before she gave me away, Her Majesty had whispered to me, "I'm giving you a very important assignment, Ocrra. Be a cheerful little teapot for my new friend, Ida, and bring her joy for the rest of her life."

Her Majesty had given me a very important job to do, and I started the adventure of a lifetime. Imagine...traveling from England to America to add joy to Ida's life.

Before the lady I came to know as Grandma Ida passed on to join Grandpa in heaven, she gave me to her granddaughter Faith. Her light brown hair and sweet smile remind me of Grandma. But Faith has bright blue eyes, very much like Her Majesty's. Every time she smiles at me, I remember both of my dear friends.

Because Faith loved Grandma so much, I became a special friend to Faith too.

Whenever she sits down for a "cuppa," as she calls it, I recall the days when Grandma used to take me out of the china cabinet and drop the Earl Grey tea leaves in me. She'd add the steaming hot water to my belly and cover me with a thick, pink cozy. A few minutes later, Grandma would uncover me and tip me over to pour out the aromatic liquid into small china teacups, which looked like miniatures of me...without a cover.

When Faith came to visit and had tea with us, Grandma would tell her of her trip to England and how I came to live in America. The way she'd give the details was special, even if we'd heard the tale a hundred times before. Faith always said she loved the story.

I still live in my china cabinet in Grandma's house because when Grandma passed away, she left everything to her one granddaughter. Faith and her husband decided to move into Grandma's Victorian house.

Faith smiles at me every day. When she has guests come to visit, she shows off my gold, pink, and deep rose-colored blooms, and then she tells them about Grandma's trip to England and why I came to America. Sometimes, I try so hard to wink at her, but I haven't figured out how to do it yet.

Now I have new friends who live with me in my china cabinet. Faith calls them Creamer and Sugar Bowl. They resemble me too with the same pattern of roses, as do my other roommates, cups and saucers. She said we're like an indoor miniature garden. We've become a very merry family in the china cabinet. Every time we get together for tea, Grandma is there with us, even if we can't see her.

Yes, Faith says I'm a special little friend and a dear one who helps her remember Grandma. Someday, her daughter will smile with the memories. I'm sure Her Majesty did, too, whenever she remembered my first home and tea party.

The day came when Faith was ready to pass me on to her daughter Rachel. Her twenty-first birthday was in five days. "I want to give her something she'd treasure forever, Ocrra."

I loved Rachel as much as I loved Faith, so I was happy.

That afternoon, Rachel stopped by to visit, but she was in a strange mood. A project at work had gone wrong, and her boss was very angry. As usual, she had come to ask her mother for advice.

Faith suggested they first have a cuppa to soothe Rachel's nerves. The young woman had always enjoyed tea with her mother and me before, but today she walked to the dining room with a big frown on her face and flicked her long blonde hair over her shoulder.

When Faith took me out of the china cabinet and set the whistling kettle on to boil, I was thrilled. The aroma of Earl Grey tea leaves would soon fill the air. Even my roses perked up their cheery colors.

Rachel stared at me with her hazel eyes and began to criticize my appearance. "Mom, why don't you just throw that old teapot out and replace it with a modern one?"

For the first time in my life, I actually let out an audible gasp.

Faith's eyes grew round as she glanced at me. She smiled. "There's no way I'd give up little Ocrra. He's been such a comfort to me all these years. There's nothing wrong with a few age marks. It gives him character."

Sure, I'm much older now than when grandma first received me from Her Majesty, but I was still in fine shape for an elderly teapot. A few hairline cracks around the rim, but...doesn't everyone get a few wrinkles around the eyes and mouth as they age? *That hurt.*

As Faith gently lifted my lid and placed the tea leaves inside my belly, Mr. Whistler sang out his song. She poured the hot water over the leaves in my belly, and the chill from Rachel's words left.

From the time Rachel was a little girl, Faith had told her the story of how I came to live in America, but she started to tell her daughter anyway. Maybe to explain how much she loved me.

Rachel stood with her hands on her hips. "Mother, if an old scrap of china means so much more to you than my advice, I'll pass on *yours...and* the cup of tea." She stomped out the door.

Faith heaved a long sigh. "It'd be useless to go after her when she's in such a mood, Ocrra. I'll have to wait until she's ready to talk to me. Perhaps she'll come back tomorrow and tell me about her problem at work."

After she'd had a cup of tea and bathed me, she sent me to bed in the china cabinet. If I could have cried, I would have. My roses turned pale and drooped. My sadness was more over Rachel's treatment of her mother than her criticism of me. Rachel had a wonderful mother—one who loved her. I'd often wished I had a mother. It hurt to see the disappointment on Faith's face.

The next day, Faith and I had tea, and she tried to explain the relationship between mothers and daughters. I learned something new. Mothers and daughters don't always see things eye-to-eye. I also learned sometimes things that transpire in a day cause a person to act out of sorts. It must have been what happened to Rachel yesterday.

Still, as Faith calmly sipped her Earl Grey from one of my little friends, a tear slipped out from under her lashes. I had so much yet to learn about human behavior.

That night, while I was fast asleep on my tea cloth in the china cabinet, a thought occurred to me. I woke with a start. Through the years, there had been times when Faith was depressed and sad, angry over something that occurred at work. She'd visit Grandma and grumble, groan, and complain.

Grandma would bring her to the kitchen and prepare a pot of tea. They'd sit and talk about what had happened. After our little tea party in Grandma's kitchen, Faith always perked up, even when she had arrived in a critical mood. Those days, the criticism never fell on me. It had fallen on other cherished items in the house.

It seems as though humans have to pick on something else, sometimes when they were angry. Did it help them forget? Grandma would be patient, and gentle, and kind with her words to Faith. Soon, the incident was forgotten.

I slipped out of the china cabinet without a sound, not an easy thing for a china teapot, mind you, and tiptoed to Faith's bedside where I whispered into her ear. "Be kind, be gentle, be patient with your daughter. Remember when you were her age and had difficult times at work and how Grandma reacted when you criticized something she loved?"

Until I was sure Faith could recall my words when she awoke, I repeated them. A few repetitions later, I slipped into the dining room, slid the window up, and let the wind carry similar words to where her daughter slept a few blocks away. "Remember the story your mother told you about how she'd have a bad day at work and visit Grandma in a foul mood? She'd criticize Grandma's house and the things she had in it. Things precious to her. And yet, Grandma never got angry. She understood and listened.

"Rachel, think of how much you mean to your mother, more than the things around her. But those objects give her pleasure when you can't be there."

I slipped back into the china cabinet and waited, very pleased with myself.

The next day was Saturday. First thing in the morning, a knock came on our door. When Faith opened the door, Rachel stepped into the foyer, head hung low. Faith threw her arms around her daughter and brought her into the kitchen. They talked, and before long, they laughed over cups of Earl Grey. My flowers shined brighter than ever.

"Mom, I don't know what I was thinking the other day." Rachel ran her finger across my roses. It tickled. "Ocrra, you are the most handsome teapot I've ever seen."

Not too bad of an arbitrator for an old teapot, am I?

Faith winked at me. I winked back. *Ha! I winked!*

The End

And be ye kind one to another, tenderhearted, forgiving one another, even as God for Christ's sake hath forgiven you. Ephesians 4:32

SPIRIT
LAKE

Spirit Lake

First published in *Dark Visions, an anthology of 34 horror stories from 27 authors*,
Copyright © 2018, Publisher : Great Oak Publishing
 Third place winner of the Word Weaver Contest, 2018

Genre: Paranormal

Patrick Nahmana and his wife take a break from Chicago city life and stay at the cabin he inherited from his Uncle Jelmer, overlooking a magnificent view of Spirit Lake. Although he loved the place when he was a child, Patrick had not visited the property for many years. The legend of Spirit Lake returned to Patrick's memory, the tale his uncle told about how the lake got its name. Had Uncle Jelmer been spinning yarns to scare him, or was the story true? They were about to find out.

Spirit Lake

Everyone says it's just a legend. *I know better.*

My name is Patrick Nahmana. I'm a mystery writer. My Uncle Jelmer had recently died and left his old log cabin on Spirit Lake to me. For weeks, my wife, Jen, had insisted on a two-week vacation away from the bustle of Chicago life. Probably so I'd pay more attention to her than my computer. So, peace and quiet beckoned as we set off for Menahga, Minnesota.

It had been years since I'd visited the cabin on Spirit Lake. It stood on the shore with a magnificent view over the water from its rough timber porch. Interlocking logs with hand-hewn notches made the mid-eighteen hundreds structure look like something out of a movie. A stone foundation, firm as the Rockies, had the letter "P" carved into one white-colored stone at the base of the back porch stairs. I had carved the "P" when my uncle first told me the cabin would someday be mine. *Branded.*

After I parked our old red truck at the cabin that midafternoon, Jen got out and gazed at the wooden structure. "It's such a big place, Patrick. Wide and sprawling." It was her first visit.

We strolled around to the back. At the porch steps, I fingered the carved initial. "This place has been in our family unchanged from its birth." I grinned at her. "I have plans to update it." We took the short stone path that meandered its way down a slope to the water.

After clearing off several inches of *partly cloudy* from the back porch early the next morning, I flipped up the hood on my jacket, sat in a lawn chair, coffee in hand, and listened to the call of blue jays. I wondered how the weatherman felt when he stepped out of his house into the snow. A resident heron flew across the water and landed in the top of a tall pine, shaking an avalanche to the ground.

Wrapped in a wool Indian blanket and carrying a huge cup of coffee, my wife stepped from the cabin onto the porch. Her short-cropped platinum-blonde hair stuck out in all directions. "Patrick, we're making a jaunt into the town of Brainerd for some early Christmas shopping today."

To distract her from the subject, I pointed to the large windows on either side of the rustic back door. "Why do you suppose there aren't any windows on the sides of this cabin? And the windows in the front are only half the size of these?"

She smirked. "Maybe the big windows in the back have something to do with that old legend." She snickered, walked back to the door, and turned. "Now get yourself out of that chair, and we'll have some breakfast."

Strategy hadn't worked. I ran my fingers through my flyaway black mop of hair and grimaced. Christmas shopping in town still on the agenda.

After breakfast, we jumped into the truck. The surprise overnight snowfall had turned the countryside into an early winter wonderland, like a fluffy white blanket covering the trees and cabin.

As I drove, Jen and I discussed gifts for family members. Actually, she suggested. I agreed. She made notes, and I traversed the blacktopped highway. During a lull in our conversation, I glanced at her. "You know, when you teased about the Spirit Lake legend this morning, it made me—"

"Don't start with that spooky story again. You know it gives me the creeps. I'm sorry I mentioned it." Her voice had a nervous quiver in it. We drove on in silence.

After we'd navigated the packed stores and endless trinkets in specialty shops well into the afternoon, Jen suggested a late lunch in a quaint café.

We sat back, having coffee at the end of our meal. "Jen, what I wanted to tell you on the way here was—"

"Can we talk about it later? That dark sky tells me we need to get back to the cabin."

She was right. It wouldn't be good to be caught in a snowstorm, not in a truck with no snow tires.

As we drove out of town, the snow began.

"Jen, we'll eventually have a family. We'll want more rooms when we vacation at the lake. Once my next book is on the market, we could pull the cabin down and rebuild. What do you think?" Jen didn't answer. Maybe she disagreed and didn't want to start an argument.

Her head turned to the direction from where we'd come, then straight ahead. "This road isn't right, Patrick. Did you take a different way back?"

After I brought the truck to a stop, I turned and scanned the area. Nothing looked the same as it had on the way to Brainerd. No other vehicles on the road. "You're right. I must have made a wrong turn. We'll go back."

A prickly sensation snaked its way up the back of my neck. The paved road had narrowed to one lane with no shoulders. When had that happened? Had I been that lost in thought about the cabin? "A turnaround is impossible here. But there's a small dirt road ahead on the left. I'll pull in."

No sooner had I pulled the truck halfway into the road, it descended at a sharp angle. We slid down the incline at an alarming speed. I pumped the brake pedal until we finally stopped with a jerk.

"Ditches on either side. I can't make a U-turn here either." We'd have to drive farther down the snow-covered road or back out. Since we couldn't see the end of the road, I decided backing out was the better of the two options.

Jen's glistening hazel eyes were huge as she peered out the back window. She braced herself with her hands on the dashboard. I stuck my head out the window and backed up. The incline seemed steeper than before. The wheels slipped from side to side in the ruts until a whooshing sound came from the open window.

She grabbed my shoulder. "What was that?"

"That, my dear, was a flat tire." At least, I hoped that was all it was.

Pitch dark, stuck in a thick stand of trees. Great! From the glove compartment, I retrieved my long-handled flashlight and slid out of the truck. The rear wheel rim had sunk deep into dirty brown snow.

The forest was silent and dark, except for the glimmer of huge falling white flakes. No yard lights anywhere. I lowered the tailgate. No spare tire. Strange. How long had it been missing? "Now what do I do?" I whispered as the hair on my neck bristled again.

Jen's half-smiling face showed through the back window. She was scared, but then, she wasn't alone. I got back in the cab.

She punched in 9-1-1 on her cell. "Wonderful! No signal."

We couldn't just sit there. "Jen, I'll walk back toward town. There must be a house along the way."

"Oh, no. You're not leaving me alone in these woods." She had that end-of-conversation expression on her face. Before I could say anything, she opened the passenger door, stepped out, and screamed as she disappeared.

My heart jumped to my throat. "*Jen.*" I pushed the driver's door open and rushed to her. She'd fallen into the ditch.

When she tried to stand, she slid further into the trench. "Oooh. Ow."

I picked her up in my arms and managed to get her back in the passenger seat. Her ankle had already begun to swell.

From the back seat, I retrieved an old T-shirt and wrapped it tightly around her foot. "Murphy's Laws have decided to take over my life." At least the comment brought a smile to her face. I hoofed it around the back end of the truck and hopped into the driver's side. "Okay. Here's the plan. I walk down this dirt road to see if any houses are nearby. You stay here and lock the doors. Keep trying your cell."

Jen latched onto my arm. "Please don't go too far. We could just stay here and wait for help."

After a quick survey, I knew no one would be coming. The muscles in my neck and shoulders tightened. My stomach had turned into a rock. "Don't worry. I won't be long."

Past the bend in the dirt road, I caught a glimpse of sky overhead between the trees. A ring circled the full moon. My Irish mother's words came to mind.

Be wary when a ring circles the moon. It's then the magic starts. Spirits roam about.

The memory caused a chill to slither up my spine. I'd never believed her superstitions back then, but the thought unsettled me. I quickened my pace.

After a stretch of thick, silent woods, little sparks of light appeared through the trees, as though hundreds of eyes watched me. Goosebumps ran over my arms and back. I began to jog.

At the end of the road, a log cabin stood barely visible in the encroaching woods. No light came from the windows. Nearby, a wolf howled, causing my scalp to prickle. I scrambled up the steps to the porch. The structure of the cabin was the same as ours on Spirit Lake, except—it looked brand new.

No one answered my knock on the door. "Hello." I crept around the raised porch to the other side of the house. At the back, two large windows with closed wooden shutters faced a dark lake. Stairs descended from the porch, and a stone footpath led to the water. Again, it struck me—everything exactly like our cabin. An eerie sense of dread engulfed me. What was happening here? Our cabin would have looked like this over a hundred years ago. "This timber smells fresh."

I continued on the path to the water's edge. The air hung still and damp. Not even a cricket chirped. No hoots or screeches from owls, no rustling from small night animals in the brush came to my ears. Only the slow, soft lap of waves on pebbles and sand.

As I stared out over the water, it occurred to me this small lake was the same size and shape as Spirit Lake. But it was surrounded by dense woods instead of an occasional house with lights shining in the evening hour. The snow had stopped, and only the moon's glow lit the night. The eerie sensation filled me again as I let my gaze run across the darkness to the far side of the water. Something moved on the distant shore. A light floated onto the surface of the lake and came straight toward me. "That can't be a reflection of the moon."

The Indian chief's daughter gasped when she saw the knife stuck into the chest of the brave whom she loved. She ran to the lake and cried that she would avenge him someday. The water splashed as she dove in. Her father watched as his daughter slipped beneath the surface before he could reach her. And that, Patrick, is how Spirit Lake got its name.

Uncle Jelmer's voice was as clear as when he'd first told the legend.

They never found her. People say they've seen her walking across the water. Searching for the killer to avenge the death of her beloved. They hear her moan.

I shuddered at the thought. Why had I ever listened to his stories?

The strange light came closer. The hair rose on my arms and neck. What looked like a knife blade flashed in the moonlight.

A wolf howled. I turned and ran.

When I climbed into the driver's seat, Jen gaped at me. I closed and locked the door.

She touched my arm. "What's wrong? Why did you run back right away? You're trembling."

"Didn't you hear that wolf?"

"What wolf?"

Her words sank in. "What do you mean, 'I ran back right away'?"

"I mean, why did you stop at the bend, turn around, and run back like something was chasing you?"

"I didn't stop. I walked clear to the end of the road."

She tilted her head and glared at me. "I kept my eyes on you the entire time, Patrick. You never went around the bend. Quit! This is no time for teasing."

"I'm not. There's a cabin by a lake down there. I knocked and called, but no one answered the door. When I went down to the water, a small light shimmered on the surface in the distance. A wolf howled—"

"*Stop it.*" Jen's eyes were like saucers as she held back tears. "That's not funny."

When I glanced at my watch, it indicated that I'd been gone for no more than ten minutes. How could that be? That trip to the lake and back had to have taken at least half an hour. My hands shook.

I slid my arm around her. "It's too dark to walk through the woods, and even if there is a house down there—my imagination must have worked overtime in this dark crop of trees. That's all."

After a couple of minutes, I turned the ignition key. The engine started but stalled. I tried again. Same result. My head dropped to the steering wheel, and I took a deep breath. Once more, I turned the key, and the engine started. After I let out the breath I'd held, I yanked the shifter into reverse. Slowly we moved backward up the incline.

Jen grabbed the dashboard. "What about the flat tire?"

"Maybe it'll keep us from sliding. I'd rather ruin the tire than stay here."

An hour later, moving backward inch by inch, we made it to the one-lane road. Still deserted. As I pulled onto the flat road, the sound of grinding on the rims made me cringe. They'd be ruined for sure. Tiny specks of light in the darkness shone through the woods and came closer. I shoved the gearshift into first and started forward.

We hadn't gone far when Jen yelled, "Stop."

I slammed on the brakes. "What?"

She pointed to another unpaved road a few yards behind us. Beyond the trees were bright lights. Why hadn't we noticed it before?

After backing up, I turned onto the road. An old service station with what looked like an antique gas pump came into view on the right. A light was on in the weathered building. Clanging filled the air and then stopped as I turned off the engine. An old man stepped out of the garage and wiped his hands on a red bandana.

He approached the truck. "What are you folks doing out so late?"

He thought seven o'clock was late? "We had a flat tire and no spare."

"No problem. I can fix that in a jiffy."

We got the wheel off, the man giving it strange looks the entire time, and he took it to the garage.

"Jen, stay in the cab. Lock the door."

Fear flashed in her eyes.

"Shore do have a newfangled truck there, boy. And here's yer problem. Ya got no inner tube in that tire. Never seen a tire like this one before."

I stared at the man, openmouthed. What kind of place was this?

"Don't know if I got one that'll fit." He walked out the back door and returned a few seconds later, shaking his head. "Nope, don't have anything that will fit this here wheel."

Nothing the guy said made sense.

The old man searched through his tools. "I might could make a repair, of sorts." He began working on the tire.

A thought struck. I rushed to the truck, where I found Jen frantically trying her phone again without success. Behind the driver's seat was a can of tire sealant. I ran back to the garage before Jen could ask anything.

The man had managed to patch the tire. I used the tire seal to reinforce the repair.

When we put the wheel back on the vehicle, I peered in at Jen. She still hadn't spoken a word, and her face had grown whiter than before.

I paid the man in cash. His brows furrowed as he looked at the bills. I climbed into the cab and rolled down the window. "Thanks for your help, sir."

"Say, you never answered why yer out so late."

Strange man. What was it Uncle Jelmer had always said? "*People used to roll up the sidewalks around here after five o'clock in days gone by.*" I snickered to myself. "We took a wrong turn and wound up on a rutted road leading to a lake and cabin."

"Where was this lake and cabin?" The old man's brows wrinkled again.

I pointed in the direction, told him about the light I'd seen on the water, and about the legend of Spirit Lake. His eyes grew large.

He came closer and whispered. "The man who stabbed that Indian was my great-grandfather. You'd best be gettin' outta here."

Was he trying to scare us? Probably good advice though. I glanced at Jen, who bit her lip.

"What did he say, Patrick?"

"Tell you later." I started the engine, made a hasty turn, and waved goodbye to the man.

Several miles down the road, everything appeared normal. We sped back to our cabin. When we arrived, I checked my watch. It was only a few minutes after eight o'clock.

As I told Jen what the old man had said, we unloaded our packages from the truck.

She slapped my arm and shook her head. "Stop trying to scare me. This trip did a good enough job." Jen hobbled to the cabin with her shirt-wrapped foot, hopped up the stairs, and disappeared inside.

I decided it'd be best to let the subject drop.

The next day, I drove into Menahga to buy a new tire and a spare. As I paid for the tires, the middle-aged man behind the counter talked about the snow.

I nodded. "Yeah, we drove through it last night. It wasn't that bad until we got lost."

"You must have gotten on a nasty dirt road, judging by the mud on that bad tire."

"I'm surprised the tire and rims weren't ruined. We wound up on a pitch-black dirt road that led to a cabin and lake." I told him about our experience and the legend.

The blood drained from the man's face. "Everyone around here knows that story, young man. The brave had won the heart of the princess, and his brother killed him out of jealousy. Word has it that the murderer's family still lives in the woods and keeps everyone away. No one's ever seen them...before maybe last night." His eyes narrowed.

"The family of the Indian princess built and still owns that old cabin on Spirit Lake. Supposed to be a sentinel of sorts to make sure the lake will always be there for the princess and her brave. Heard tell they're never supposed to sell the property or even do anything to change it. Some kind of—Indian curse involved." The man handed me the receipt.

"As far as the Indian princess goes, it's only when she walks without her brave you need fear her."

Dad never told me that Nahmana was an Indian name. I thought we were Scandinavian.

We still visit Spirit Lake and still own the old cabin, unchanged. Guess we always will, considering. But—we make sure to pay attention to where we're driving, and we always keep an eye out on the lake.

Never have seen the princess again. Occasionally, we'll hear someone say they saw her walking in the woods with her brave. I'm *really* happy about that.

The End

Peace I leave with you, my peace I give unto you: not as the world giveth, give I unto you. Let not your heart be troubled, neither let it be afraid. John 14:27

About The Author

Raised in Illinois, Sharon K Connell went to school through college classes in Chicago. She has also lived in Missouri, California, Florida, Ohio, and now resides in Texas. Her travels have taken her to all but six states in the United States. She has also visited Canada and Mexico.

Sharon is a member of the American Christian Fiction Writers organization and the Houston Writers Guild. She runs the Facebook Christian Writers & Readers Group Forum and puts out Novel Thoughts, a monthly newsletter for writers as well as readers.

A graduate of the Pensacola Bible Institute in Florida, Sharon has studied the Bible from cover to cover. She writes stores about people who discover God will allow things in their lives to bring them to a saving knowledge of Jesus Christ and/or increase their faith.

Her certificate in fiction writing was received from the International Writing Program through the University of Iowa.

The short stories within this book were written are in a variety of genres, but her primary genre is Christian Romance Suspense.

Let the words of my mouth, and the meditation of my heart, be acceptable in thy sight, O Lord, my strength, and my redeemer. Psalm 19:14

Links

Website: www.authorsharonkconnell.com

Amazon Author Page:
http://www.amazon.com/author/sharonkconnell

Author's book page on Facebook:
https://www.facebook.com/averypresenthelpbook1

Author's Page on Facebook:
https://www.facebook.com/ChristianRomanceSuspense/

Group Forum on Facebook:
https://www.facebook.com/groups/ChristianWritersAndReadersGroupForum/

Twitter: https://twitter.com/SharonKConnell

Goodreads: https://www.goodreads.com/SharonKConnell

LinkedIn: https://www.linkedin.com/in/sharonkconnell

Pinterest: https://www.pinterest.com/rosecastle1/

Other Works

Novels
A Very Present Help
Paths of Righteousness
There Abideth Hope
His Perfect Love
Treasure in a Field

Novella
Icicles to Moonbeams

Short Stories in Anthologies
Ding-A-Ling Holiday Blues
In Tales of Texas, Vol. 2

Spirit Lake
In Dark Visions

Thank you for Reading

Made in the USA
Monee, IL
08 November 2020